The Case of the Famished Parson

George Bellairs (1902–1982). He was, by day, a Manchester bank manager with close connections to the University of Manchester. He is often referred to as the English Simenon, as his detective stories combine wicked crimes and classic police procedurals, set in quaint villages.

He was born in Lancashire and married Gladys Mabel Roberts in 1930. He was a devoted Francophile and travelled there frequently, writing for English newspapers and magazines and weaving French towns into his fiction.

Bellairs' first mystery, *Littlejohn on Leave* (1941) introduced his series detective, Detective Inspector Thomas Littlejohn. Full of scandal and intrigue, the series peeks inside small towns in the mid twentieth century and Littlejohn is injected with humour, intelligence and compassion.

He died on the Isle of Man in April 1982 just before his eightieth birthday.

ALSO BY GEORGE BELLAIRS

The Case of the Famished Parson
The Case of the Demented Spiv
Corpses in Enderby
Death in High Provence
Death Sends for the Doctor
Murder Makes Mistakes
Bones in the Wilderness
Toll the Bell for Murder
Death in the Fearful Night
Death in the Wasteland
Death of a Shadow
Intruder in the Dark
Death in Desolation
The Night They Killed Joss Varran

The Case of the Famished Parson

An Inspector Littlejohn Mystery

George Bellairs

This edition published in 2016 by Ipso Books

First published in 1949 Great Britain by John Gifford Ltd. and in the Unites States, by Macmillan Co.

Ipso Books is a division of Peters Fraser + Dunlop Ltd

Drury House, 34-43 Russell Street, London WC2B 5HA

"Which distractions do not only unman men, but they run them upon desperate ventures, to obtain they know not what."

JOHN BUNYAN.

CONTENTS

Chapter One
The Tower Room

WEDNESDAY, September 4th. The Cape Mervin Hotel was as quiet as the grave. Everybody was "in" and the night-porter was reading in his cubby-hole under the stairs.

A little hunchbacked fellow was Fennick, with long arms, spindleshanks accentuated by tight, narrow-fitting trousers—somebody's cast-offs—and big feet. Some disease had robbed him of all his hair. He didn't need to shave and when he showed himself in public, he wore a wig. The latter was now lying on a chair, as though Fennick had scalped himself for relief.

The plainwood table was littered with papers and periodicals left behind by guests and rescued by the porter from the salvage dump. He spent a lot of his time reading and never remembered what he had read.

Two or three dailies, some illustrated weeklies of the cheaper variety, and a copy of Old Moore's Almanac. A sporting paper and a partly completed football pool form. . . .

Fennick was reading "What the Stars have in Store." He was breathing hard and one side of his face was contorted with concentration. He gathered that the omens were favourable. Venus and Jupiter in good aspect. Success in love affairs and a promising career. . . . He felt better for it.

Outside the tide was out. The boats in the river were aground. The light in the tower at the end of the breakwater changed from white to red and back at minute intervals. The wind blew up the gravel drive leading from the quayside to the hotel and tossed bits of paper and dead leaves about. Down below on the road to the breakwater you could see the coke glowing in a brazier and the silhouette of a watchman's cabin nearby.

The clock on the Jubilee Tower on the promenade across the river struck midnight. At this signal the grandfather clocks in the public rooms and hall began to chime all at once in appalling discord, like a peal of bells being 'fired.' The owner of the hotel was keen on antiques and bric-a-brac and meticulously oiled and regulated all his clocks himself.

Then, in mockery of the ponderous timepieces, a clock somewhere else cuckooed a dozen times. The under-manager, who had a sense of humour, kept it in his office, set to operate just after the heavy ones. Most people laughed at it. So far, the proprietor hadn't seen the point.

Fennick stirred himself, blinked his hairless eyelids, laid aside the oracle, stroked his naked head as though soothing it after absorbing so much of the future, and rose to lock the main door. Then he entered the bar.

The barmaid and cocktail-shaker had been gone almost an hour. Used glasses stood around waiting to be washed first thing in the morning. The night-porter took a tankard from a hook and emptied all the dregs from the glasses into it. Beer, stout, gin, whisky, vermouth. . . . A good pint of it. . . . One hand behind his back, he drank without stopping, his prominent Adam's-apple and dewlaps agitating, until it was all gone. Then he wiped his mouth on the back of his hand, sighed with satisfaction, selected and lighted the largest cigarette-end from one of the many ash-trays scattered about and went off to his next job.

It was the rule that Fennick collected all shoes, chalked their room-numbers on their soles and carried them to the basement for cleaning. But he had ways of his own. He took a large newspaper and his box of cleaning materials and silently dealt with the footwear, one by one, as it stood outside the doors of the bedrooms, spreading the paper to protect the carpet.

Fennick started for the first floor. Rooms 1, 2, 3, 4 and 5, with the best views over the river and bay. His gait was jaunty, for he had had a few beers before finally fuddling himself with the dregs from the bar. He hummed a tune to himself.

Don't send my boy to prizzen,

It's the first crime wot he's done. . . .

He tottered up the main staircase with his cleaning-box and stopped at the first door.

Number I was a single room. Once it had been double, but the need for more bathrooms had split it in two. Outside, on the mat, a pair of substantial handmade black shoes. Fennick glided his two brushes and polishing-cloth over them with hasty approval. They belonged to Judge Tennant, of the High Court. He came every year at this time for a fishing holiday. He tipped meticulously. Neither too much not too little. Yet you didn't mind. You felt justice had been done when you got it.

Fennick had been sitting on his haunches. Now and then he cocked an ear to make sure that nobody was stirring. He moved like a crab to Number 2 gently dragging his tackle along with him.

This was the best room, with a private bath. Let to a millionaire, they said. It was a double, and in the register the occupants had gone down as Mr. and Mrs. Cuhady. All the staff, from the head waiter down to the handyman who raked the gravel round the hotel and washed down the cars, knew it was a lie. The head waiter was an expert on that sort of thing. With thirty years' experience in a dining-room you can soon size-up a situation.

That was how they knew about the honeymoon couple in Number 3, too. Outside their door was a pair of new men's brogues and some new brown suede ladies' shoes. "The Bride's travelling costume consisted of . . . with brown suede shoes . . . ." Fennick knew all about it from reading his papers in the small hours.

There were five pairs of women's shoes outside Number 2. Brown leather, blue suede, black and red tops, light patent leather, and a pair with silk uppers. All expensive ones.

Five pairs in a day! Fennick snarled and showed a nasty gap where he had lost four teeth. Just like her! He cleaned the brown, the black-and-red and the patent uppers with the same brushes for spite. The blue suede he ignored altogether. And he spat contemptuously on the silk ones and wiped them with a dirty cloth.

Mr. Cuhady seemed to have forgotten his shoes altogether. That was a great relief! He was very particular about them. Lovely hand-made ones and the colour of old mahogany. And you had to do them properly, or he played merry hell. Mr. Cuhady had blood-pressure and "Mrs." Cuhady didn't seem to be doing it any good. The magnate was snoring his head off. There was no other sound in Number 2. Fennick bet himself that his partner was noiselessly rifling Cuhady's pocket-book . . . .

He crawled along and dealt with the honeymoon shoes. They weren't too good. Probably they'd saved-up hard to have their first nights together at a posh hotel and would remember it all their lives. "Remember the Cape Mervin . . . ?" Fennick, sentimental under his mixed load of drinks, spat on all four soles lor good luck . . . . He crept on.

Two pairs of brogues this time. Male and female. Good ones, too, and well cared for. Fennick handled them both with reverence. A right good job. For he had read a lot in his papers about one of the occupants of Room 4. An illustrated weekly had even interviewed him at Scotland Yard and printed his picture.

On the other side of the door were two beds, separated by a table on which stood a reading-lamp, a travelling-clock and two empty milk glasses. In one bed a good-looking, middle-aged woman was sitting-up, with a dressing-gown round her shoulders, reading a book about George Sand.

In the other a man was sleeping on his back. On his nose a pair of horn-rimmed spectacles; on the eiderdown a thriller had fallen from his limp hand. He wore striped silk pyjamas and his mouth was slightly open.

The woman rose, removed the man's glasses and book, drew the bedclothes over his arms, kissed him lightly on his thinning hair, and then climbed back into bed and resumed her reading. Inspector Littlejohn slept on . . . .

Fennick had reached the last room of the block. Number 5 was the tower room. The front of the Cape Mervin Hotel was like a castle. A wing, a tower, the main block, a second tower, and then another wing. Number 5 was in the left-hand tower. And it was occupied at the time by the Bishop of Greyle and his wife.

As a rule there were two pairs here, too. Heavy, brown serviceable shoes for Mrs. Bishop; boots, dusty, with solid, heavy soles and curled-up toes, for His Lordship. Tonight there was only one pair. Mrs. Greyle's. Nobody properly knew the bishop's surname. He signed everything "J. C. Greyle" and they didn't like to ask his real name. Somebody thought it was Macintosh.

Fennick was so immersed in his speculations that he didn't see the door open. Suddenly looking up he found Mrs. Greyle standing there in a blue dressing-gown staring down at him.

The night-porter hastily placed his hand flat on the top of his head to cover his nakedness, for he'd forgotten his wig. He felt to have a substantial thatch of hair now, however, and every hair of his head seemed to rise.

"Have you seen my husband?" said Mrs. Greyle, or Macintosh, or whatever it was. "He went out at eleven and hasn't returned."

Fennick writhed from his haunches to his knees and then to his feet, like a prizefighter who has been down.

"No, mum . . . I don't usually do the boots this way, but I'm so late, see?"

"Wherever can he be . . . ? So unusual . . . ."

She had a net over her grey hair. Her face was white and drawn. It must have been a very pretty face years ago . . . . Her hands trembled as she clutched her gown to her.

"Anything I can do, mum?"

"I can't see that there is. I don't know where he's gone. The telephone in our room rang at a quarter to eleven and he just said he had to go out and wouldn't be long. He didn't explain . . . ."

"Oh, he'll be turnin' up. P'raps visitin' the sick, mum."

Fennick was eager to be off. The manager's quarters were just above and if he got roused and found out Fennick's little cleaning dodge, it would be, as the porter inwardly told himself, Napooh!

It was no different the following morning, when the hotel woke up. The bishop was still missing.

At nine o'clock things began to happen.

First, the millionaire sent for the manager and raised the roof.

His shoes were dirty. Last night he'd put them out as usual to be cleaned. This morning he had found them, not only uncleaned, but twice as dirty as he'd left them. In fact, muddy right up to the laces. He demanded an immediate personal interview with the proprietor. Somebody was going to get fired for it . . . .

"Mrs." Cuhady, who liked to see other people being bullied and pushed around, watched with growing pride and satisfaction the magnate's mounting blood-pressure . . .

At nine-fifteen they took the bishop's corpse to the town morgue in the ambulance. He had been found at the bottom of Bolter's Hole, with the tide lapping round his emaciated body and his head bashed in.

The first that most of the guests knew of something unusual was the appearance of the proprietor in the dining-room just after nine. This was extraordinary, for Mr. Allain was a lazy man with a reputation for staying in bed until after ten.

Mr. Allain, a tall fat man and usually impurturbable, appeared unshaven and looking distracted. After a few words with the head waiter, who pointed out a man eating an omelette at a table near the window, he waddled across the room.

They only got bacon once a week at the Cape Mervin and Littlejohn was tackling an omelette without enthusiasm. His wife was reading a letter from her sister at Melton Mowbray who had just had another child.

Mr. Allain whispered to Littlejohn. All eyes in the room turned in their direction. Littlejohn emptied his mouth and could be seen mildly arguing. In response, Mr. Allain, who was half French, clasped his hands in entreaty. So, Littlejohn, after a word to his wife, left the room with the proprietor . . . .

"Something must have happened," said the guests one to another.

Chapter Two
Bolter's Hole

HARRY KEAST was quite a character locally. He had been drawing old-age pension for two years. Before that, he had been out-porter at Port Mervin ra-ilway station and graduated through the horse-and-cart stage to running an old Ford truck. When Harry got his pension he sold-out and became a hanger-on at the golf club. Sometimes he helped with the mowing machines; sometimes he acted as caddy.

At 7.30 one morning Harry turned up at the links. There was nobody about. Not even the groundsman. The dew was heavy on the grass and as you walked across it, you left a trail of footprints behind.

Keast made a practice of being there early in the season. He had a nose like a gun-dog for golf balls. First thing in the morning he found most of the balls abandoned the day before by despairing players. Besides, on holidays you give up the search earlier, for you value every minute of the game. Money doesn't seem to matter much then, so what's an odd ball or two . . . ?

Harry was a little thin man with a thick white thatch covered by a cloth cap. He often wore the peak front to back. He had a ragged moustache, hollow, tanned cheeks, pale blue twinkling eyes and a neck toughened and wrinkled like leather from exposure. He had little or no formal education, but experience and shrewdness made up for a lot. He was fond of long words, but knew hardly any. So he made them up as he went along for the sheer pleasure of mouthing them.

"Brognostication is the thief of time," he said to himself by way of excusing his early appearance on the links.

With a stick, Keast pounded the tussocks of the rough and dislodged a number of balls. He was like a man searching the roosts for eggs. He knew all the spots and hardly ever came empty away. He gathered a fair lot of mushrooms, too, and filled a carrier bag with them. More than ten bob a pound in the shops in town!

From the centre of the ninth fairway the seabirds rose crying. They soared around, glided to earth and vanished, as though the earth had ejected and swallowed them up again.

There was nothing mysterious about the phenomenon. This was Bolter's Hole, one of the hazards of the game.

At Bolter's Hole the sea suddenly makes a concentrated rush inland for quarter of a mile. In their tireless search for flaws in the coastline, the waves have found this thin wedge of soft rock and with all the time of geology at their disposal have crept farther and farther inland until, at last, reaching hard rock, they have been forced to turn and retreat.

That is what you think when you reach Bolter's Hole. A long, narrow gorge flanked by jagged walls of rock about a hundred feet high. It looks deeper than that. At the ebb a quiet retreat for sun-bathing, for the floor is covered in pale sand. At full-tide almost like a little inland lake. The sea enters by a thin neck at great force, expands, rushes on and then, encountering the bastion of hard rock about a quarter of a mile farther on, boils and whirls in anger, thrashes itself into flying foam and finally retreats with a drag which sucks all the flotsam around through the portal into the open ocean.

The fury of the waves where the solid rock turns them about has worn a sort of amphitheatre in the middle of the land, in shape something like the bulb of an old pneumatic motor-horn with the tube as the gorge leading out to the sea.

"Obsequious portentatiousness," said Harry Keast expressing to himself his awe at the sight. He surveyed the grandeur of the cliffs, with the gulls flying to them and then rising with wild cries as though the earth had shaken them off.

With an expert eye the solitary figure examined the place. The tide was out and the time was ripe. If you weren't long and sure on number nine your ball went right in Bolter's Hole. Of course, if you didn't care to risk it, you could play a dog-leg and avoid the hazard. But most players took the risk and prayed for a good ball, and if it didn't come off, blamed something else. Unfamiliarity with the course, or even the face of somebody passing by. Never their own bad play . . . .

Harry had on special occasions found as many as thirty good balls in the Hole after a bad day. Those which landed square on the beach were soon drawn to kingdom-come at the ebb. But the rocks and seaweed caught a lot . . . .

The watcher was looking at some rocks and seaweed just below the normal tide-line. A small fissure running down to the floor of the Hole began in a spongy ledge, with a crack in the middle. From the fissure projected what looked like a pair of boots.

"Idiosyncratic circumstances," said Harry and began to scramble down the face of the cliff to investigate. He was nimble for his years and wore nailed boots for the job. He was soon there.

What Harry saw made him whistle. Head downwards, suspended by its boots, which were wedged in the top of the fissure, was a long, thin body. In its present position, it looked longer than ever.

The aged caddy's vocabulary temporarily gave out, and then, death seemed to stimulate him to a religious effort.

"'oly Nebuchadnezzar!" was all he could say.

He touched the body and found it cold. The face was *to* the bare rock, but he turned it sufficiently to see the gaunt, pale-green features, the craggy jaw, the heavy, thick-based nose, and, beneath them, the clerical collar and coloured episcopal front.

The back of the head had been smashed in by some terrible blow or other . . . .

Sadly Harry surveyed the corpse for a moment.

"Itchabod!" he said, scrambled up the rocks, stood on the edge of the Hole for a moment and looked back at the corpse, and repeated himself.

"H'itchabod."

Then he hared off to the golf house.

He knew where there was an easily opened window. He entered and rang-up the Mervin police.

"Come instantaneously," he shouted by way of speeding them.

Littlejohn explained that he was on vacation. Mr. Allain knew that already, for he himself had invited Littlejohn and his wife to stay there.

Allain had kept a restaurant on Tottenham Court Road until the bombing reduced it to nothing and sent him scuttering to the distant seaside for a quieter time. In the old days the Littlejohns had been good customers and the Inspector had helped Allain a time or two. Especially in the matter of getting naturalised . . . .

"I only want you to take a watching brief for the hotel, Inspector. I feel safe if you're about. The local police . . . "

And he shrugged his shoulders to show how badly he thought of them.

Allain might have been the head of an asylum through whose guilty negligence half the inmates had escaped and met their deaths, instead of an hotelier not responsible for what his guests did when off the premises.

"But it's very awkward, Mr. Allain. I'm a police officer, not a private investigator. It just isn't done . . . . One policeman trespassing on another's territory . . . ."

But when the Port Mervin police did arrive, it was in the shape of Superintendent Bowater. He and Littlejohn had met and liked one another in a case miles from Port Mervin, when Bowater had been an Inspector in a colliery town. So that made it easy. Bowater was only too glad of the unofficial help.

Mrs. Littlejohn was annoyed. Her husband was already overworked. He fell asleep from fatigue here, there and everywhere, and then talked in his sleep. That was why she had come with him to look after him. She had never before been absent from one of her sister's frequent accouchements . . . .

Chapter Three
The Dirty Shoes

FOR a brief spell Mr. Cuhady kicked up such a fuss about his shoes that the murder of the bishop took a back seat.

The millionaire had a large mouth brimming over with gold teeth and he trumpeted his lamentations and threats all over the place. He demanded an apology and a new pair of shoes from the owner of the hotel, refused to disclose the maker or the price of the old ones, and then had to be assisted to his room through blood pressure. There he remained sulking and expecting apoplexy all day . . . .

It was Mrs. Littlejohn who mentioned the affair of the magnate's footwear when her husband returned to lunch from police headquarters. Littlejohn calmly enjoyed his meal and then, borrowing the shoes from the hotel manager with whom Cuhady had left them after trying to fling them at his head, he took them to the scene of the crime and discovered that the murderer had worn them. The footprints which marked the signs of scuffling on the cliffedge tallied with Mr. Cuhady's soles.

They did not break the news at once to the magnate, fearing cerebral haemorrhage might carry him right off . . . .

But before that, Littlejohn had been hard at work with the police.

Superintendent Bowater had done a lot of hemming and hawing about Littlejohn's status. The Chief Constable was a stickler for etiquette and the Superintendent felt he might treat Littlejohn as an interfering amateur if things weren't put on a proper footing. So it was agreed that Scotland Yard should be officially called-in. Littlejohn thus found himself on a busman's holiday and his wife was more irritated than ever. Bowater tried to console her by saying her husband would only be called upon in a consultative capacity on odd occasions, but Letty was not impressed. She had heard that tale before . . . .

The police station seemed full of people. Two doctors, the hotel proprietor, several policemen, a handful of officials, including Littlejohn, and finally, Mr. Cuhady who had called to demand an immediate enquiry into the disappearance of his shoes. Harry Keast was there, as well. They couldn't get rid of Harry. He kept telling his tale over and over again.

"I was gathering golf balls . . . . A caddy, I am, you know, and that's extraneous to my job . . . ."

It took rather a long time to get statements from all the parties concerned. A young constable typed them straight from dictation. He was very patient. He abridged the lengthy ones and skilfully translated Harry Keast's homemade English into something like sense.

Mrs. Macintosh, the bishop's wife, was stunned by the news and a short statement was taken from her at the hotel.

Briefly, the information boiled down to this.

At a quarter to eleven on the night of the crime, the telephone rang in the bishop's room. Dr. and Mrs. Macintosh had only just entered and had not started to undress. The bishop answered the call, told his wife he had to go out, put on his hat and coat and went off without saying where he was going.

Bowater, who took down the statement, had gently pressed Mrs. Macintosh for some reason for this strange behaviour.

Had she not asked who was ringing at that time of night? Hadn't she even enquired where her husband was going so late?

Yes, she had. But her husband seemed preoccupied and apparently didn't hear her questions. He was very absent-minded sometimes when problems troubled him. All he had said was, "I must go out for a little while and will be back soon . . . ."

"Was your husband in the habit of doing this sort of thing?"

Mrs. Macintosh had looked bewildered and a bit startled.

"No . . . ."

"Had he been worried of late?"

"He seemed very worried. But I think it was overwork. That was the reason for our taking the holiday . . . ."

Bowater and Littlejohn were going through the statements in the calm of the Superintendent's room. Outside, you could hear a sergeant trying to control the turmoil caused by witnesses and others.

"I got the impression, somehow, that the bishop's lady wasn't telling the full tale. Not that I think she was lying. She'd be above that. But holding a lot back. Sort of knew more than she cared to tell . . . ."

Bowater was a tall, fat, clean, hairy man. Short dark moustache, bushy black eyebrows, bald head with the hair from one side long and plastered across it, and large, dark, protruding eyes. The backs of his huge hands were covered in thick black hair . . . .

Littlejohn liked him. He was a modest man and made no bones about being out of his depth in a case of this sort.

"So that was all you got from her?"

"Yes. But, as I said, I'd the idea she might have theories of her own. She seemed so completely bowled over, though, that I couldn't press matters further . . . ."

"And the next who saw the bishop, with the exception of the murderer, of course, was Keast . . . ."

You could still hear Keast's voice raised in the next room. They couldn't get rid of Harry. He seemed to think that the bottom would drop out of the investigation if he cleared off.

"There he was hangin' perpendiculous down the cliff. Face to the wall, as you might say . . . ."

Bowater shuffled his papers.

"Keast found him head down, feet wedged in a sort of crevice or crack in the rock. And now look at what the two constables and the sergeant say who went to investigate . . . ."

"The body hung head downwards, face to the rock, held rigid because the feet were firmly wedged in a crack in the rock. We had difficulty in freeing it . . . ."

"What do you make of that?"

"Well, Superintendent, it looks to me that if the body hadn't been caught that way, we might easily have thought it was an accident."

"Exactly. That blow might have been caused by the head hitting the rock. But, as it seems the reverend gentleman went over the top *facing* Bolter's Hole, he couldn't have caught the back of his head unless he performed a sort of cart-wheel."

"Right. So reconstructing the crime we get . . . ?"

"Somebody hit the bishop on the head and pushed him over the cliff. Whoever did it, probably thought he'd fall right to the bottom. Next ebb tide the body would float off and be found anywhere. The blow on the head might have been through catching anything a hard knock . . . ."

"Yes . . . ."

"But pushed over face first, the bishop slides down the rocks instead of hurling to the bottom and his boots get caught firmly in the . . . the . . . fissure. Nowhere could he have caught the back of his head. So the fracture was by a blow delivered by somebody whose cunning little plan failed . . . ."

"Q.E.D."

"Beg pardon?"

"That's what we wanted to prove. It was murder . . . . You're probably right, Superintendent."

There was an imperative rap on the door and the police surgeon sauntered in. A thin, self-important, busy little man. Port Mervin was too small to boast an exclusive police surgeon of its own. Dr. Tordopp was a general practitioner as well and thought no small beer of himself. He was serious, casual and a bit patronising, and immaculate. He looked to have come out of a bandbox instead of the morgue.

"I've finished," he said testily as though washing his hands of the police and all their works.

"We'd better see the body, then," said Bowater. "Coming, Inspector?"

"I'll stay here," snapped Tordopp. "There's some tea coming and God knows I need it. I'll be here when you've finished, if you aren't too long . . . ."

Littlejohn followed Bowater out. On the way the Superintendent spoke to one of the constables.

"Keep Tordopp's tea back till we return," he said peevishly. "We'll want some too after what we're doing. Tordopp can wait . . . ."

The mortuary adjoined the police-station. A white-tiled little place recently built. Its gruesome contents reposed in large oven-like cupboards along one wall. The attendant wheeled out the remains of the Bishop of Greyle on a trolley.

"Nasty!" said Bowater and neither of them spoke again until they left the place. The attendant cheerfully busied himself about the room, opening the oven-like receptacles and looking in, like a baker inspecting the last lot of bread. He whistled happily between his teeth.

Littlejohn was used to this sort of thing, but when Bowater deftly turned back the sheet which covered the body, he felt a wave of horror surge over him. The man was a walking skeleton! His eyes met those of his colleague and he could see the Superintendent was thinking the same. The face had a greenish palor and to add to the ghastliness, Tordopp, in his wisdom, had transversely sawed the head in two and neatly wired it together again. The clean-shaven lips were drawn back in an awful grin, a *risus sardonicus.* The wound at the back of the skull had been cleaned. But it was deep. A desperate blow which had pierced to the brain . . . .

"Gosh!" said Bowater when they got outside. "Looks as if the bishop expected what was coming to him and as though the murderer meant him to have it . . . ."

Tordopp was drinking his tea when they returned to Bowater's room. There were two cups on the Superintendent's desk, too. The surgeon had been out and played merry hell at the delay in bringing the brew.

"Hi, Lancaster! How many times have I told you not to put cups of tea on the leather of my desk?" shouted Bowater to a bashful young officer who seemed to be official caterer. "It leaves rings and you can't get 'em off . . . ."

"I put them there," snapped Tordopp with great relish and he gave the Superintendent another *risus sardonicus,* more appalling than that of the corpse.

Bowater let it pass

Tordopp removed his long, narrow red nose from his cup. He suffered from dyspepsia which he couldn't cure. It coloured all his life and greatly embittered him.

"He was killed outright by the blow on the head," he said tersely.

Bowater couldn't resist a thrust. He removed his large bulbous nose from a thick teacup, like a rhinoceros surfacing.

"Did you need to saw off the top of his head to find that out?"

"Leave my business to me, please. It ill becomes you to meddle . . . ."

They looked ready for a real set-to.

Littlejohn intervened.

"I never saw a body so emaciated . . . . I mean a body of one in his position in life . . . ."

Tordopp gave another sour smile.

"I was just going to say when Bowater started teaching me my business, that I gave the body a more than usual overhauling. It interested me. There was nothing wrong with the organs. In fact, it was a first-class life. Except that he was undernourished. Just famished, I'd say . . . ."

"But why . . . . ?"

The Superintendent addressed the surgeon aggressively, as though Tordopp held the secret and wouldn't disclose it.

"How should I know? That's your business. I'm not running round the town asking why the bishop was undernourished. Better ask his wife."

Tordopp finished off his tea, meticulously placed his empty cup and saucer on the leather part of Bowater's desktop, gave him another *risus* and put on his small bowler hat.

"I'll send in a written report this afternoon. Good day to you . . . " he yapped and closed the door with a bang of finality.

"Jumped-up bloody little snoot," murmured the Superintendent under his breath and catching Littlejohn's eye, flushed and cleared his throat apologetically.

"Fennick's here, sir," said the bashful young constable, entering awkwardly. To tell the truth, he had never encountered Scotland Yard before and was quite overcome. Since the age of five he had been a feverish reader of thrillers and aspired to be a detective himself one day. But not in Port Mervin!

"Taken his statement?"

"Yes, sir."

"Let me have it then. Oh, and send Fennick in."

Fennick looked annoyed and in bad shape. He worked by night and slept by day and they had routed him from his bed to make a statement. The sergeant-in-charge had given him a good telling-off for taking so long in getting up and putting in an appearance.

"What's the matter with you, Fennick? You look annoyed."

The night porter wasn't in the least put out of countenance by the police. Goings-on after dark at a large fashionable hotel had long-since disillusioned him. He could tell you a thing or two about some famous ones he'd come across . . . .

"Not damn-well good enough. I got to get me sleep in the day. Workin', I am, while you lot's in yer beds. How the 'ell am I to do me job proper if you lot get me up as soon as I'm in bed. And all fer nothin'. I don't know nothin'. 'Ow should I?"

"Keep a civil tongue in your head, you," snapped Bowater. "You were on duty, or should have been, when the bishop left the hotel. Just answer a few questions properly and then you can get back to bed, if that's where you *are* going . . . ."

"Of course that's where I'm goin.' Where else? A chap's got to 'ave his sleep. You lot . . . "

"Shut up!"

Littlejohn smiled to himself. He'd never met such a quarrelsome crew!

"Now, Fennick, answer my questions and show a bit of sense. The sooner we get through 'em, the sooner you'll get back to bed . . . ."

"I can't tell yer anythin' . . . ."

"Leave me to judge that. First, did you see the bishop go out of the hotel between quarter to eleven and eleven o'clock?"

"No, I didn't . . . ."

"What time do you go on duty?"

"Ten. But I ain't a sort o' sentry, you know. Don't say ''oo goes there?' to all as come an' go, if that's what you're after. I got me duties to do . . . ."

"Such as?"

"Answer the 'phone, stoke up the boilers, odds and ends of messages for those as 'as things they want after ten; an' believe me there's a 'ell of a lot of 'em sometimes . . . ."

"Yes, yes. What were you doing at the times I mentioned last night?"

"Can't reckerlect . . . ."

Fennick obviously wasn't trying.

"Come on now, that's enough of that. You're deliberately obstructing the police, Fennick, and that's a punishable offence. So get cracking and think hard."

Littlejohn looked at Fennick's moron face. Question whether he *could* think, let alone think hard.

Suddenly, for some reason, the porter's face lit up. Like putting another shilling in the gas-meter.

"Yes," he said with serious cogitation. "Come to think on it. Yes, I stoked-up the fire about a quarter to eleven."

"How do you know it was that time?"

Fennick's jaws rotated like someone chewing tobacco. He looked ready to spit. It seemed in some-way connected with his process of thinking.

"Bar closes at eleven. I looked at the clock. Yes, I looked at the clock, I did. Quarter of an hour to go, I sez to myself. Just time to feed the boilers. So I did."

"Why were you interested in the bar closing?"

Littlejohn smiled. Fennick's cloudy eyes caught the Inspector's own and he cast at the detective a look of understanding hate.

"I *ain't* particular interested. I jest thought that, I did."

"H'm. How long were you in the boiler house?"

"About ten minutes. They'd been a lot havin' baths agen. Wot the 'ell they always want to be in the bath for, I don't know. They'd drawn a 'ell of a lot of water off, so I 'ad to draw the damper and 'ot it up. Took out the cinders and clinkers, raked 'er up a bit, and put more coke on . . . ."

"You were back before eleven?"

"Yes."

"How do you know that?"

"Oh, 'ell. How much more?"

Try as he would, the Superintendent couldn't budge Fennick on that point. He *knew* it wasn't eleven and that was that. The mechanism and evidence whereby he knew weren't plain. They all centred round that last mixed drink in the bar, but Fennick didn't disclose that.

"Oh, very well. Let's get on . . . ."

"'urry up then. I want to get to me bed . . . ."

"All in good time . . . ."

Bowater was sadistically enjoying himself.

"You didn't see the bishop go out?"

"No. I said so once, didn't I? NO."

"Did you see *anybody* go in or out about that time?"

"No. There was a few in the bar and they one and all stopped there till it closed. They allis do. A few as had been to the pictures got in about ha' past ten. They all went up, else in the bar. After that lot, I see nobody till I come up from the fire-hole . . . ."

"The what?"

"Boiler 'ouse."

It was hopeless. Fennick was too stupid to be a good witness. If he saw anyone he'd probably forgotten.

"Who looks after the telephone after the day staff leave?"

"Me."

"It's in the hall-porter's quarters, isn't it?"

"Yes. When 'e goes 'e changes the buzzer to a bell and I can hear it from where I am . . . ."

"Except when you aren't there . . . ."

"Well. Can't be in two places at once't, can I?"

"Were there any incoming calls after half-past ten that night?"

"No."

"Sure?"

"No. Positive."

"But there might have been while you were downstairs tending the fire?"

"No. If a call comes in, the bell keeps on ringing, even if they ring-off. That is, unless you turn off the bell. I don't do that. Can't. Don't know how. If you want ter stop it, you lifts your own receiver. Then it stops and stays stopped till somebody else rings. See?"

"I see. If you wanted to call one of the rooms, you could do that from the switchboard?"

"Of course. One room can speak to another that way, too."

"H'm."

Bowater turned to Littlejohn.

"Looks as if somebody spoke to the bishop from the board, then, doesn't it?"

"Yes," said Littlejohn.

"And you, Fennick, saw nothing peculiar at all that night?"

"Only Mrs. Bishop huntin' for her husband. Came out askin' about him as I gathered up the boots to clean 'em . . . ."

Outside there was a great commotion. Angry yoices raised and somebody thumping a desk.

The young constable tapped on the door and entered.

"Mr. Cuhady's here again, sir. It seems he wants to see the night porter about his shoes. The hotel manager's with him. They've been to Fennick's house and they told them he was here . . . ."

Fennick didn't seem moved. He was so bewildered by the turn of events and the apparent importance of himself in the case that he had given up the problem in despair. He expected the sack for it. So why bother? There was a dearth of night porters so he could soon get another job. He shambled out to face the storm.

The frustration of not getting at the facts about his dirty shoes had become a monomania with the magnate. He was going to get Fennick sacked if it cost him every penny he'd got.

"Hi' you . . . . That's the man," trumpeted Cuhady. "You there . . . ."

"Put a sock in it," yelled Fennick and walked past him to the door and home to bed.

They had to help Mr. Cuhady to a chair and give him a drink of water.

The result was that, unable to get night men for love or money, the manager pretended to sack Fennick to please Cuhady. In other words, the night porter got holiday with pay till the magnate had packed up his traps and departed with his hired woman.

But there was one more event before the scene at the police station closed that morning.

Judge Tennant arrived and asked to see the Superintendent. When he presented his card, a great hush fell on the place. Just as when he entered his court, fully robed, at the assizes.

"Judge Tennant," said the sergeant-in-charge to the attendant constables and they all sprang to attention.

Harry Keast removed his cap, rather a difficult feat, for it was on back to front, shambled to the door, and beat it to the golf links like someone evading the millstones of the law.

"Good morning, Superintendent," said the judge.

Littlejohn was introduced.

"Good morning to you, Inspector. We've seen each other before, haven't we? I'm glad you're here. It will help things . . . ."

"Yes, won't it?" said Bowater beaming. He didn't know what else to say.

"I've called about the death of the Bishop of Greyle. An old and dear friend of mine. His wife is very distressed and, I'm afraid, won't bear much questioning for some time to come. So I promised her I do all I could to ease her burden."

"Very good of you, I'm sure, my lord."

"So," said the judge, sitting back nonchalantly in the hard wooden chair. "Is there any way in which I can help?"

It was a funny situation. It seemed a judge's place to ask the questions. However . . .

In the outer room, Mr. Cuhady was being helped off to his huge car. He hadn't cut much ice at the police station and was out for new blood.

"I'll write to the Home Secretary about this," he shouted as a parting shot.

As the car slid away, he was still bawling threats, bullying the attendant hotel manager and sacking his chauffeur.

But nobody seemed to care.

Chapter Four
The Boy Who Got On

SIR FRANCIS TENNANT was a tall, lean man with very long legs. He sat with them crossed before him and indicated that he was at the service of the police officers.

The judge was a bachelor. Nobody knew why. He never took anyone into his confidence, newspaper files were singularly thin in details of his life and the standard books of personal reference contained only the bold outlines of his legal career. On the bench his summing-up to the jury was always a masterpiece of precision. He never added a lecture to a sentence and his court was well-known for the courtesy and good manners which he insisted should always prevail in it.

"If there is anything you wish to know about the late bishop, I shall be pleased to tell you, if I can."

Bowater looked at Littlejohn. He seemed at a loss how to begin.

"This is a strange affair altogether, sir," said the Inspector. "How comes it that an apparently harmless church dignitary should meet such a violent end? And premeditated, too, by the look of it. Could he have had any enemies sufficiently ruthless to want to kill him?"

"I'm as baffled as you are, Inspector . . . ."

There was nothing of the legal hawk about the judge. His features were round and firm, his colouring good, and his nose small and straight. He hadn't even the traditional gimlet eyes and thin lips. A very benevolent face, in fact. Tired a little about the kindly grey eyes, but otherwise like a cleric himself, with a calm spirit.

"Were you a personal friend of the dead man, Sir Francis?"

"Yes. I've known him all my life. We attended the same school. In fact, we were born in the same village, Medhope in Glebeshire."

"Perhaps, then, you wouldn't mind giving us some details of Dr. Macintosh's life . . . ."

"You could get a lot from *Who's Who,* I've no doubt. For the rest, his parents were large farmers. He was always a clever lad and got on well. I didn't see much of him till we went to school in Glebechester. My own home was actually in the centre of the village. The Macintosh farm was a few miles out."

"Were they Scots?"

"By extraction, yes. But three or four generations of them had farmed Cranage, as the place was called. The bishop's aged mother is still alive and lives there with her son and daughter."

"Have you any ideas of your own as to what might be the roots of this tragedy, sir? It must have been brewing for some time. The bishop was called-out late at night to what was obviously a premeditated fate . . . ."

"It seems so. His wife has no idea what it was all about. She is as puzzled as we are. She can think of nobody who might have wished him ill . . . ."

"How did Dr. Macintosh stand in church circles?"

The judge rubbed his short, round chin.

"Um. Just so-so, I fear. Initially, a good preacher and a brilliant organiser, Macintosh quickly attracted the attention of his superiors. He made rapid strides at first. Then, suddenly, was becalmed in mid-career. Greyle is a small bishopric. Everyone expected him to go higher very quickly, Instead . . . . Well, he's been there, let me see . . . Twelve years, at least."

"Why?"

"If you'll look up his career, you'll find that Macintosh first qualified as a medical man. I don't think he'd any intention of going into the profession. I never talked with him about it. I was studying for the bar when he was at medical school. But I gather he had the view that a parson ought to have first-rate knowledge of the body to be able to get at the soul . . . ."

"I see. So he took medicine before divinity, sir?"

"Yes. And I have an idea that there's where he's come up against his superiors. At first, and as an ordinary clergyman he showed a great flair for organising and the true ministry. His churches, both in the East End of London and in large towns in the provinces were crowded and prosperous. But it was a mistake to take him from active parish work to the sedate calm of a cathedral city. A great mistake. It turned him in upon himself . . . ."

"In what way, sir?"

"The Dean of Greyle will be here soon. You'd better get a fuller story from him. But I can say that Macintosh's old medical zeal came back to him as he found time to return to it. He took up psychiatry with zest. Even to the extent of neglecting his episcopal duties."

"With what end in view? Merely as a spare-time occupation?"

"Certainly not. A conscientious bishop hasn't any spare time. Macintosh had a theory, probably right, that a religious revival would come from the spirit and that healing the spirit was the first task of the church. He wrote two or three books on it . . . ."

"Oh. It's that Macintosh is it, sir? I'd no idea. His books are in all the booksellers' windows."

"That's the man. Of late, he's been overdoing it. Working too hard on his hobby-horse. Worn himself out. If this had been suicide, I could have understood it . . . ."

"We can't see how it could have been."

"So I gather."

"We've just inspected the body, sir. We were amazed at the emaciation . . . . The bishop is just a bag of skin and bone."

"Worked himself to nothing, I suppose."

"I don't know. He looked starved . . . ."

The judge smiled urbanely.

"Hardly that. Times are bad, I grant, but surely . . . ."

"That's what it looked like, all the same. And the police surgeon seems to think so, too. The man was famished."

"Well, if there's nothing more, I'll get back to my lunch. I merely called to avoid Mrs. Macintosh being troubled at a time like this. I'm quite at your disposal, however . . . ."

"We thank you for your help, sir. For the present, I don't think there's much more you can do for us. The information's been most useful."

"Much obliged, I'm sure," added Bowater, who had been quiet throughout the interview.

So, Sir Francis Tennant left them and Littlejohn was not long following him to the hotel.

There the Inspector was faced with the incident of Cuhady's shoes. And he found that whoever had scuffled with the bishop on the edge of Bolter's Hole had worn them.

Naturally, Littlejohn's first thought was of Cuhady. But the hotel manager warned him not to mention the shoes, to say nothing of Cuhady's wearing them when he thought they were being cleaned. It would be enough to cause a violent eruption. Nevertheless, Littlejohn decided to beard the magnate in his den. He was conducted with reluctance to the royal suite.

Cuhady refused to see Littlejohn at first. When he heard about the shoes, however, he changed his tune. He thought they'd brought in Scotland Yard to appease him and said he would see the Inspector right away and what the hell were they waiting for.

"Glad they've got somebody proper on the job. I'm a business man myself and like things done slick," barked Mr. Cuhady. He had a voice like a fox terrier. He was sitting in an armchair with a bottle of seltzer water at his elbow and a box of pills beside it. "Mrs." Cuhady was hovering round. She and the magnate were pals again. When the blood drummed in the millionaire's ears at times of pressure, he got terrified. He wanted somebody to tell him he wasn't going to die. That is where the pseudo-Mrs. Cuhady came in.

"Like a drink, Inspector?"

"No thanks, sir. Not on duty."

"Have a cigar. No? Put a couple in your pocket then. They're the best. Now. Let's get on. What about my shoes?"

"Well, sir, they've become involved in a murder case . . . ."

"'Ere. What the hell . . . ."

Mrs. Cuhady, arranging some flowers, or pretending to do so, turned.

"Now, Teddy-bear, keep calm, dear. You know what the doctor said."

"To hell with the doctor, and don't call me Teddy-bear! What's all this about murder, Inspector? Why can't I have a bit of peace. Every little thing that happens to me grows into a big one . . . ."

He was almost weeping with sorrow for himself. Mr. Cuhady had stored up his wealth in barns and storehouses and was ready to eat, drink and be merry and then the Lord had smitten him with blood-pressure. Just after he'd built a church, too, and endowed a chair in Moral Science at a University. It wasn't good enough . . . .

Littlejohn very quietly told the magnate all that had happened. Black dots swam before the millionaire's eyes again and his ears drummed like a bugle band.

"You mean to tell me, whoever killed the reverend put on my shoes to do it? I . . . I . . . "

Cuhady sprang to his feet, strode up and down, pawed the air, flung his arms about and then collapsed on the couch. "Mrs." Cuhady rushed to his side and patted him gently.

"There, there. It's nothing. Only an old pair of shoes. You can buy some more . . . ."

"I don't want to buy some more . . . . I feel very poorly, Grace. Why do they keep tormenting me . . . ?"

Grace patted and soothed the magnate until he became himself again.

"He's that worried," she explained to Littlejohn, especially for the millionaire's benefit. "Everybody takes advantage of him. And he's such a generous, kind-hearted darling once you get to know him . . . ."

Mr. Cuhady was lapping it up and smiling sheepishly like a soothed baby-in-arms.

Littlejohn nearly wanted to be sick.

He wanted to ask Cuhady what he was doing at the time of the crime, but feared another explosion, perhaps a fatal one this time.

Who were you with last night, so to speak!

He compromised.

"I suppose you were both together all last evening?"

Grace gave Littlejohn a look which was a complete answer. She wasn't going to let Cuhady out of her sight after nightfall while he'd a penny left in the bank, if she could help it!

"Of course," said Cuhady. "My little Grace's the only friend I've got in the world . . . . Here, What the hell?"

Mr. Cuhady had all the cunning of the commercial rat. He smelled danger.

"You meanin' to say I might have worn my own shoes and done for the reverend. That what you're getting at? Because if you are . . . "

"No, no. I'm naturally interested in all that went on on this floor last night. Have you any useful suggestions?"

"No. I'm interested, too. I came to bed at ten-thirty; asleep ten minutes later. Remember nothing till this morning when I woke to this mess. What a day!"

"In that case, I'll not trouble you further. Thank you."

"So, that means that whoever killed the reverend took my shoes, does it?"

"I guess it does, sir."

"Then I hope you catch him quick, and he swings for it . . . . I . . . I . . . "

"Now, now, my pet . . . . Remember what the doctor said. What would happen to Gracie if her Cuhad-daddy made himself ill . . . ?"

The magnate almost started to guggle and gurgle.

"What indeed," thought Littlejohn and left them prattling to one another like a couple of kids.

Downstairs, Bowater was questioning the barmaid and the cocktail-mixer. Littlejohn joined him.

The shaker was pure Nordic, with curly blonde hair and a quiff across it like a horizontal question mark.

No. He hadn't seen anything the night before. There wasn't a soul about. He'd seen the bar emptied and closed. Everybody had melted away and the place was deserted when he said good-night to Fennick and Evelyn.

Evelyn was the barmaid. She lived in. Dark, buxom and bossy, with blonde hair. She'd overdone the peroxide and only needed pink eyes to look like an albino.

"Yes, the lot," concurred Evelyn and patted her blonde waves to make sure they were still there.

"Yes," reiterated Gus. "And Old Shearwater was too drunk to help himself, so Father O'Shaughnessy nearly carried him to bed. Dr. Rooksby was three-sheets in the wind, too, and Mrs. Dyson-whatsisname was very merry."

"Were any of them in a condition to notice *anything*?" said Littlejohn.

"The priest was O.K. Steady two-pinter he is."

"Maybe he can tell us something," muttered Bowater. "Though it's a forlorn hope. Still, he might have been interested. Bishop in a rival church, you know."

A look of owlish profundity crossed the Superintendent's face.

"Religious murder?" grinned Littlejohn.

"Might be."

Bowater looked a bit hurt at his colleague's levity.

"Here, Evelyn, bring the Superintendent and me a pint apiece," said the Inspector. "We'll go off duty for a minute or two."

Bowater, judging from the look on his face, thought it a good idea.

"Did you meet anybody on the way to bed, Evelyn?" asked Bowater.

"Not a soul."

"Did either of you see anybody go in the hall-porter's room to telephone?"

"No."

Littlejohn reminded Bowater that the telephone message was made before eleven. The bar didn't close till eleven.

"I was just coming to that," replied the Superintendent with a sheepish gleam in his eye.

"Did anyone leave the bar, perhaps to telephone, between say, ten-thirty and when you closed?"

"No. There was a nice fire and they were all sat round. Evelyn and me carried round the drinks. There were only about six there, having their nightcaps and none of 'em moved till we called Time."

"This is a do," said Bowater plaintively. "Nobody's seen anybody."

"We'd better have the names of everybody who was in the bar at the time," said Littlejohn. He picked up an old menu card and took out a pencil. "Now, Gus," he said to the cocktail expert.

Gus and Evelyn went into conference and finally recited all the names between them.

Mr. Sharples. Dr. Rooksby. Mr. Hennessy. Old Shearwater. A chap called Wentworth. That McWhinnie bloke. The chap who always had half a pint of Bass and half a pint of Guinness mixed for a nightcap, think his name's Hoyle or Doyle. Mrs. Dyson-Forbes who always likes sitting drinking with the men. Oh, and don't forget Father O'Shaughnessy, a priest on holiday, who enjoys a pint with the next and plays billiards like a professional."

"That all?" said Littlejohn.

"Yes," said Gus.

Chapter Five
The Card Players

LATE in the afternoon a gale sprang up and whipped the sea into a fury. Heavy clouds scudded across the sky and pouring rain drenched the town. The row of tall trees planted in front of the hotel to break the weather tossed and swayed to and fro in unison, tortured by the wind.

Everybody stayed in the hotel, except an eccentric regular who lived a life of clockwork routine and couldn't change his plans. He struggled down the drive clad in oilskins and inclining his body to resist the gale. On the quay the harbour-master in sou'wester and waterproof was rushing around making arrangements for a number of boats, standing off the coast, to come into the shelter of the river. In the far distance a small vessel seemed in distress . . . .

The lounge was full. Mrs. Dyson-Forbes was taking tea with three other women. Two of them were knitting and another was clutching a book. Their eyes were all over the place, sizing-up the other women, watching the men, whilst at the same time they maintained their conversation. Now and then they called each other darling, smiled or looked poisonous as the talk flowed on, and followed each other's moves like intent chess players.

Most of the tables were taken when Littlejohn entered the room. He had left his wife with an elderly woman in the smaller resident's lounge where they were talking about arthritis. The elderly woman was a martyr to it and Mrs. Littlejohn's father had suffered from it years ago . . . .

Littlejohn could see at once who were the notables of the place, for the small-fry eyed them with deference and followed their conversation respectfully.

Several people nodded affably to Littlejohn. His reputation had gone round. Mrs. Dyson-Forbes's gang smiled at him and then drew their heads together to whisper.

"Good looking . . . ."

"Wouldn't think he was a detective . . . ."

" . . . his wife's hat?"

At a table under the large bow-window four men were playing cards. They monopolised the place as though it were their own. They were residents and generally treated casual visitors with contempt. One of them, with his back to the window, saw Littlejohn enter and with a word to his friends, rose and approached.

"Inspector Littlejohn? My name's Sharples . . . . I live here. Used to be in London . . . Knew some of the chaps at Scotland Yard. I hope you'll make yourself at home . . . ."

A little, prancing fellow with a round, smooth baby face and bright blue eyes. He was a bit of a lady-killer and was trying to make an impression on those present.

"Come and join us . . . . We've just finished a hand of cards. Have a drink . . . ."

He put his arm round Littlejohn's shoulders. It was a bit of an effort for him. They might have been pals all their lives.

"This is Dr. Rooksby . . . . Lives here, too, and has consulting rooms in town. Anything wrong with your eyes, ears, nose or throat, he's your man . . . ."

The doctor looked at Sharples with a sneer of contempt. Then he smiled at Littlejohn and showed a number of gold teeth. A flabby, bouncing man, dressed in formal black coat and grey trousers. He wore rimless spectacles and his eyes were shifty.

"Glad to know you, Inspector. How's the case coming on . . . ?"

The hand he offered was soft and dry and as you squeezed it gently there was no bone resistance. The boneless wonder?

"And Mr. Hennessy . . . ."

A long, craggy face, with folded skin round the mouth and chin. Close-set eyes and long nose, slightly askew. He wore check tweeds of a horsy cut and looked like a racecourse tout.

"Pleased to meet you . . . ."

The voice was harsh and nasal.

"Mr. Hennessy's living here for the summer. His wife's on the Riviera, so he's shut up house . . . ."

Sharples kept prattling on. The rest looked bored with him.

They found a chair for Littlejohn and ordered him a drink. They'd all been drinking whisky and Sharples looked half-seas over.

The fourth member of the party smiled at the Inspector.

"I'm Wentworth . . . ."

His voice drawled; he seemed half-asleep, but his eyes beneath heavy lids were taking everything in. He looked like Hollywood's idea of an English butler. Impassive face, firm mouth, white linen and unassuming dark suit. A bowler hat would have finished the picture.

"I'm sorry, Wentworth . . . ."

He sniggered. The slight might have been deliberate, or baby-face might have grown tired before he reached Wentworth.

There was a pause.

"Bit of a blow being saddled with a case like this in the middle of your holiday, eh?" chuckled Sharples. His fishy eyes roved round the room, halted for a moment on a well-dressed woman who was entering and lit up as he showed his teeth in a grin at her.

"Yes, rather . . . ."

Littlejohn didn't know what to say to them. The whole party looked bored to death. He wondered what they'd have done if the weather had been fine. His right hand still felt cold after Wentworth's icy grip . . . .

The whole business was dismal in the extreme, but it had to be gone through. All four of them had been up and drinking in the bar on the night of the crime. Apparently a drinking, card playing gang of moneyed men, bored to death and tired even of each other.

The women sat around in a state of armed neutrality and tension. Many of them looked with disapproving eyes and pursed lips at Sharples's well-dressed friend, who sailed through them with marvellous poise and unconcern and settled beside a tall thin man with a toothbrush moustache, half-open mouth and vacant expression. He at once straightened his tie, grimaced with pleasure, and turned on his charm.

" . . . Seemed a quiet unassuming chap, though a bit on the standoffish side. Couldn't get him into conversation. But to want to murder him . . . It's fantastic . . . "

Sharples was laying down the law owlishly. He might have been trying to prove that the murder hadn't occurred at all.

"But he *was* murdered. So what are you bothering about? Somebody did it."

Hennessy was petulant and ready to go elsewhere and do something else, if there had been anything else to do and anywhere else to go. But there wasn't . . . .

"H'm . . . h'm . . . h'm . . . "

Dr. Rooksby pursed his lips and looked wise. He didn't seem to have any views on the subject and seemed anxious to change it.

"Lily! . . . What'll it be?"

"Four whiskies, Lily . . . "

Wentworth didn't speak. He considered his bluish filbert-shaped nails with a frown.

"But they say somebody rang up the bishop to meet them and then murdered him. Have you found out who did the ringing-up, Inspector?"

Rooksby looked for all the world as if he were giving Littlejohn the key to the mystery.

"No, doctor. But it seems the call was put-in from the switchboard here. Now, you four gentlemen were in the bar at the time that call was made. Did any of you see or hear anything that might be connected with it?"

Sharples had finished his drink already. Surprising that such a soak kept so young-looking.

"So you've learned that?"

Rooksby gave a nod of approval as though congratulating Littlejohn.

"No. We were all together and didn't stir from the bar fire till closing time. That's so, isn't it?"

The other three nodded agreement with Sharples. Hennessy put his hands deep in his trousers pockets, stretched his legs and yawned. He held his glass up to the light, closed one eye as he looked through its contents, and then drank it off.

"Sorry. Don't see how we can help you. It's just as Sharples says . . . " he said stiffly. He was eager to be rid of Littlejohn and get on with the card playing.

"There were some others with you, I hear . . . ."

"Yes. McWhinnie, a commercial traveller, who left this morning. He never stirred from the fire. Calls here for a day or two every quarter on his rounds. Has a good job and makes plenty . . . . Electrical goods, I think . . . " Sharples knew all about it.

"Yes . . . Doyle, the solicitor was up with Mrs. Dyson-Forbes. He's her lawyer. They sat in the bar till closing time, too. And then there was . . . let me see . . . Shearwater, who lives here and that priest fellow. O'Shaughnessy, I think . . . . The padre saw Shearwater to bed . . . . One over the eight. Couldn't move under his own power . . . ."

Sharples guffawed, rose, preened himself and smiled at another woman.

"That's all we know . . . ."

Littlejohn rose. All eyes turned on him. As though he were going to make an immediate arrest. It was a bit embarrassing. And to mend matters, Mrs. Littlejohn appeared. Eyes swivelled in her direction then. Hopefully, as though she were going to question her husband publicly. The women sized-up her clothes and stared from her to Littlejohn as though trying to sense whether they were a happy couple or not . . . .

"Thanks for the drink, gentlemen, and for your information. I think I'll try and find Father O'Shaughnessy. Where will he be, can you say?"

Sharples knew.

"Like as not in the billiard-room. Billiard mad. Never saw such a chap for the ivories."

Littlejohn was glad to get away from them. And they seemed glad to see the last of him, too, and get back to their bridge. Stakes were high ones and their thirst for gambling was second only to that for alcohol.

"Lily . . . Same again . . . ."

There was something amiss with that lot, thought Littlejohn. Eager to know the latest developments, yet as close as clams. Maybe it was just that they resented intrusion. After all, his brief interlude with them probably held up the transfer of several pounds in stakes.

"Have you had tea, Tom?"

"No. Have yours alone, will you? I'm just off to find a priest."

Mrs. Dyson-Forbes seemed able to read their lips or their thoughts.

"Come and join us, Mrs. Littlejohn, won't you?"

Letty's eyes met her husband's.

"Thank you for nothing," he read in them behind the ironical smile.

The billiard-room was in the basement and lit by artificial light under great green shades. Two tables, a small bar and padded green seats round the walls. Both tables were occupied and the priest and his friend were playing snooker at the one near the bar. On a marble topped little table nearby stood two half-empty glasses of whisky.

Father O'Shaughnessy was small, portly and urbane. He had a round pink face, childlike blue eyes behind round, gold-rimmed spectacles, and an aura of well-scrubbed cleanliness. The first thing you noticed about him was his hands. Large, white, eloquent and unctuous. Made for comforting, blessing, fastidiously handling the Elements, and skilled in manipulating a billiard cue.

Click!

Father O'Shaughnessy shot the green ball smartly in the pocket. Then he turned with an almost apologetic look to his opponent and saw Littlejohn.

"Ah! I'd been expecting you, Inspector, sooner or later."

"Why, father?"

They shook hands.

And Father O'Shaughnessy gently recited to Littlejohn the train of reasoning which had brought the Inspector down into the underworld of the hotel to see him.

The good father wasn't quite so innocent as he looked!

Meanwhile, the opponent had badly fumbled a shot and shuffled round to join the other two. He was tall, heavy, grey and sad-looking and his clothes hung on him as though he had undergone recent shrinkage.

"Mr. Shearwater, Inspector."

Shearwater extended a large, white, dry hand with little or no grip in it.

Father O'Shaughnessy intimated that he would talk to Littlejohn between his shots on the table. To tell the truth, they had a billiard-table at the presbytery where the priest lived, and his friend, the Canon, beat O'Shaughnessy every time. He had made up his mind that if possible, he would return from his holiday and give the Canon a licking! And he wasn't wasting any time.

Click! Thud! Into the pocket again.

"Yes. I saw our friend here to bed last night. He needed a bit of help and guidance . . . ."

"Did you see anyone about on the way, sir?"

"Yes. Judge Tennant coming from the bathroom, in pyjamas, bath-robe and with sponge-bag. Irritating our good friend Fennick by using-up the bathwater."

"Anyone else?"

"No, Inspector."

"You can assure me that the following people were in the bar and didn't stir until you and your friend left?"

Littlejohn showed the priest his list of names.

"Yes. They were all there. That's right. As you say."

Shearwater fumbled another shot and grumbled under his breath. His face was a mask. Never a smile, but never a scowl or frown. Just impassive. He only seemed half-alive. He was drinking more than the priest, too.

"And you left Mr. Shearwater at his door, sir?"

"Took him in . . . . And pulled off his shoes for him. He hardly knew what he was doing. For all I know, he might have thrown himself on his bed and slept in his clothes. Did you Shearwater?"

"What?"

"Did you sleep in your clothes after I left you last night?"

"Certainly not. I was quite able to undress myself, wash, and clean my teeth and do everything a respectable man should do."

The voice was quiet and cultured.

The honeymoon couple were playing on the other table. The husband, with many terms of endearment, was instructing his wife in the art of billiards. He wasn't much good himself, but she pretended not to notice.

"Now try for a cannon, darling . . . ."

They resented Littlejohn's intrusion. The bar was closed, so there were no spectators. And with two preoccupied fogies on the other table, it was just like being alone. Then, Littlejohn descended upon them and spoiled it. It was too bad. If they'd known what a tactful legion in himself Father O'Shaughnessy was, they'd have thought differently perhaps.

"Now get in off the cush, honey . . . ."

"I suppose you want to know about the telephone, too, Inspector. As we passed the porter's room someone was using the telephone there."

This was amazing! Perhaps, given time, the priest would say who killed the bishop!

"Did you see who it was, father?"

"No. There was a light on and I heard someone say 'Hullo.' That's all."

"Did you recognise the voice?"

Father O'Shaughnessy sorrowfully watched Shearwater bungle another shot and then drove the black home for game.

"Yes."

"Young Michael, the porter's boy. I don't know whether or not he'll be able to help you, but you might try him."

"I will, sir. And many thanks."

"See you again, Inspector. Good luck to you. And keep an eye on that crowd who play cards in the lounge. I don't like that lot. There's something unholy about the syndicate. Another game, Shearwater?"

The honeymoon couple were squabbling as Littlejohn left. She had accused him of petulant play because she wasn't a good learner!

Father O'Shaughnessy turned reproachful round spectacles upon them. They were spoiling his game!

Chapter Six
Gaiters

THE inquest was adjourned. That was a foregone conclusion. The Deputy-Coroner, a young solicitor in local practice, officiated in the absence of the Coroner on holidays. Harry Keast seemed to be chief witness. It was Harry's day out. He wore a faded navy-blue suit, carried an outmoded bowler-hat and was hardly recognisable. The Deputy-Coroner was very kind to him. Harry had carried his clubs for many a mile across the links.

Keast went into great detail and the Deputy bore patiently with him. It became a sort of informal confab. between them.

"You know Bolter's Hole, sir. Driver, brassie on the ninth and you're over. You've done it many a time, sir . . . ."

"Yes. You walked straight there, Keast?"

"Yes, sir. Straight as the drive you generally get . . . . An' I stopped at the first bunker. Sometimes a ball or two lost in the rough near there and there's a mushroom or two sometimes in the proximity . . . ."

"Yes . . . ."

And so on.

Dr. Tordopp, who was waiting to give evidence and digesting with difficulty a very simple meal, looked ready to murder the pair of them. When his turn came, he was very terse and *to* the point. The bishop had been killed outright by a savage blow on the head. He reeled off a lot of highly technical jargon with great relish and venomously translated it into simple speech at the request of the awe-struck foreman of the jury, who kept shuffling in his seat, for he was anxious to be getting back to his shop.

The widow was there flanked by two clerical gentlemen, both wearing gaiters. When they put in an appearance a great hush fell on the court, partly out of sympathy for the bereaved, partly out of spurious reverence, because the two clergymen seemed to bear the dusty air of a cathedral about with them. Somebody sniggered. The Dean of Greyle was small and chubby, the Venerable Archdeacon of Greyle tall and thin. Filing down the gangway they reminded you of a penny-halfpenny or else a velocipede.

The diocesan solicitor, a fusty elderly gentleman in a threadbare morning coat splattered with snuff, accompanied the party. He was there to represent the cathedral interests. He spoke for the bishop's widow, who was too distressed to answer questions. His name was Rufus Flank.

Mr. Rufus Flank's voice was worn out, like his clothes. He began *fortissimo* and gradually diminuendoed until at the end of each sentence you couldn't hear a word he said. Then he cleared his throat with a strange hawking sound and began again.

"MISSIS MACINTOSH TOO DISTressed . . . speak on behalf . . . regret unable . . . light . . . Hrumph, chmha . . . THEREFORE BEG the court . . . indulgence . . . . Hrumph, chmha . . . ."

"Speak-up, can't you?" said someone at the back of the court, mistaking it for a theatrical performance or a political meeting.

The jury turned like one man to the coroner, their questioning eyes beseeching his aid.

Dr. Tordopp was heard acidly saying that he hadn't all day to spare and had a surgery full of patients waiting for him. The dean eventually leaned over to the solicitors' table and in a voice like whipped cream persuaded Mr. Flank to lift up his head and open his mouth which Mr. Flank did, greatly to everybody's relief.

The inquest got nobody anywhere, except it permitted the bishop's body to be released for interment and gave the police the shelter of an adjournment behind which to pursue their enquiries.

The Deputy expressed his sympathy and condoled with the church in the loss of so eminent a dignitary, and then crossed the road to the courts to defend a farmer who had been watering his milk. The jury went to their offices and shops feeling they had done a good job and grumbling about Mr. Flank. Mr. Flank joined the cathedral undertaker in a sumptuous Rolls-Royce hearse and went off to claim the body. And the dean and venerable archdeacon, having placed Mrs. Macintosh comfortably in a rather small car, got in themselves with great difficulty, one having a verticle struggle and the other a horizontal one, and drove off to the hotel for lunch and to gather luggage.

The bright spot in Littlejohn's morning was the arrival of Sergeant Cromwell, for whom he had sent, and who met him on the steps of the hotel. Cromwell looked quite in keeping with the ecclesiastical scene for he was dressed, as usual, like a cathedral verger. Behind him, in the hall was the huge suitcase he always carries however short his visit. It is always heavy and only Cromwell and Littlejohn know what the sergeant carries in it. *Inter alia,* books on police law, forensic medicine and toxicology, domestic medicine, wild birds and celebrated murder cases. Cromwell doesn't believe in being caught on the hop . . . . There is a chest-expander, too, and occasionally, two revolvers, ammunition and handcuffs!

Young Michael the page-boy had tried to lift the case and given it up as a bad job. Littlejohn captured Michael and took him aside.

"Now, my lad, what's your name? Michael? Well, Michael, I want a word or two with you . . . ."

Michael looked ready to panic and flee. The hall-porter had already told him all about Littlejohn and urged him to mind his P's and Q's. His knees began to knock, his mouth dried up and his voice completely disappeared.

"Yes, sir," he finally managed to get out.

"On the night the Bishop of Greyle died, I've been told you answered the hotel telephone just before you went off duty. Is that so, Michael?"

Littlejohn was using the lad's Christian name, otherwise Michael would have expected immediate arrest. He wondered confusedly what crime might lie behind the simple job he usually performed at that time.

"Yes, sir. I did. But I didn't do nothin' . . . ."

"Nobody's saying you did, Michael. I'm not trying to blame or frighten you. I'm wanting your help . . . ."

That was better! Michael's face began to shine and the cloth of his tunic strained at the fourteen little buttons down the front of it.

"Yes, sir. I answered it. For the bishop it was. I wanted to tell you, but the hall porter said it was my place to speak when I was asked and not before. I was to remember my place, sir . . . ."

"Oh, he did, did he? Well, you can tell me about it now, Michael."

"There's not much to tell, sir. About a quarter to eleven the 'phone went. It's my duty to answer it between the hall porter going and the night porter coming on. Then I can go to bed."

"I see. The 'phone went. Then what . . . ?"

"It sounded from a 'phone box, sir . . . ."

"Why?"

"Well, we're not on the automatics here, yet, and I heard the operator say to the bloke . . . the man who was ringing, 'Your call, go ahead . . . .'"

"Yes?"

"Then the man spoke to me. 'Who is that?' he says. 'Cape Mervin Hotel,' I says. 'Who is speakin'?' he says. I says the hotel name again. Then he gets mad and shouts, 'But who is it?' So I says: 'The page, who do you want?'"

"Go on, Michael."

The boy was standing to attention like a private being questioned on parade.

"Then the bloke says, 'Now listen. Now listen. I want you to give the Bishop of Greyle a message. Tell him to come to Bolter's Hole at once where he-knows-who will meet him and show him what he wants to see.' Just like that, he said it. And then he made me tell him back what he said. So I did. And then he says, 'Give it him over the telephone in his room and let me hear you do it.' So I did. It's easy. Just leave the switch open and speak on another line."

"You're a bright lad, Michael. Then what?"

"I told the bishop over his bedroom 'phone. He just said 'Right' and hung up, as though he'd been expecting it."

"And the caller heard you do it?"

"Yes. And when I'd done he says, 'Good boy,' he says. 'Now, if you'll look at the bottom of the railing just opposite the hotel entrance on the quayside, you'll find half-a-crown for your trouble.' Must have been a decent bloke, becos I found the money."

"H'm. Yes."

Then Michael suddenly seemed to realise that he might have been giving the murderer a good character and turned pale. He saw himself as an accessory.

"All right, Michael. Don't worry. You only did your job and you've helped me no end. What sort of a voice was it?"

"A man's, sir. Muffled, it sounded. But well-spoken. That's all I can say."

"Did you see the bishop go out?"

"No, sir. Fennick came on then, so I went off for my supper."

Littlejohn handed Michael another half-crown. The page was so inspired and exhilarated by his co-operation with Scotland Yard, that in a sudden access of strength he seized Cromwell's bag and, puffing and groaning happily, tumbled it up the two flights of stairs to the second-floor-back where the Sergeant had been given a room usually allotted to chauffeurs and body-servants by the snobbish management.

Littlejohn had arranged to see Mrs. Macintosh before her departure, so after lunch, he went to a private room assigned to her and her friends by the sympathising director. There he found her flanked by the Dean and Chapter, in the form of the Venerable Archdeacon.

Before he entered, Littlejohn could hear the buzz of clerical voices in the room. The dean opened the door in response to his knock and the first thing he saw was Mrs. Macintosh, her face red and swollen, drying her eyes with a handkerchief. There was on the faces of the two clergymen that upset expression, that look of righteous sorrow which follows the giving of a large dose of heart-balm. They had been thoroughly disturbing poor Mrs. Macintosh by sympathy and sentimentality, when they ought to have been taking her mind from her grief.

The bereaved woman was small and fragile, with a tired nervous face and grey hair. She must have been very dainty and beautiful in her young days and probably very vivacious, too. Now she was utterly stricken.

The dean, round, pink and boisterous in normal circumstances, was in a mood for tiptoes, shushing, drawn blinds and comfortable unction. He greeted Littlejohn in a hushed, lathery voice, reduced to a whisper.

"Ah, Inspector. Come in. I trust this interview will not be long and that you won't distress the widow. This has been a great shock to us all . . . . The bishop was my best friend . . . ."

"I certainly won't cause any further grief to Mrs. Macintosh, sir, and assure you I'll be as brief as possible."

"Good, good. Come along then."

The long-limbed, lean archdeacon rose to meet Littlejohn. His voice was terse and rasping, with a strange musical resonance. He was about sixty with a bald head and tufts of white hair over his ears. A fine, scholarly face, perhaps a little coarsened by self-indulgence maybe in food and drink. He, too, spoke softly.

"Good afternoon, Inspector. Pray be brief, so as not to distress the dear lady. A sad loss, we've suffered. I was the bishop's best friend, so if I can help . . . " he said, whilst the dean's back was turned as he sought another chair.

An ecclesiastical Codlin and Short!

They had been treating Mrs. Macintosh like a frail museum specimen not to be roughly handled, but she was having none of it. She rose to greet Littlejohn and he felt a glow of admiration and sympathy as he shook the hand she offered him and looked at the strained, kindly face, full of grace and character.

Mrs. Macintosh was not going to allow the two men to cast her for the part of a helpless, incoherent weakling if she could avoid it.

"Please sit down, Inspector," she said. "And do not hesitate to question me as fully as you think fit. Vengeance won't, I know, bring my husband back, but you have a duty to perform and I wish to help you in every way to do it . . . ."

"Thank you, madam. I can't tell you how much I regret the need for troubling you at a time like this and how much I sympathise with you in your loss and grief. First, may I ask if you knew who rang up your husband and for what purpose?"

"I have not the least idea, Inspector. He didn't tell me and had not mentioned anything previously which gave me any idea what it was all about. There were parts of his duties which he never discussed with me . . . ."

Somehow, Littlejohn got the impression that though the bishop and his wife might have been comfortably married, there wasn't a great deal of warmth and intimacy in the relationship. And remembering the austere, frosty look of His Lordship in death, Littlejohn was not surprised. Of course, alive, the bishop might have been warm and genial, but somehow . . . .

The two cathedral dignitaries were sitting near, saying little but nodding, smiling, gesturing to show their interest and desire to help.

The atmosphere of the room was chill and depressing. Carved oak panels covered the walls from top to bottom and the place was very high. It gave you the feeling of sitting at the bottom of a funnel.

"Had he any enemies that you were aware of, Mrs. Macintosh?"

"Certainly not. He was very well-liked by all who knew him and for anyone to wish to do him violence was unthinkable."

The two clergymen nodded agreement and made noises of concurrence.

"As his best friend and intimately in his confidence, I can assure you on that point, Inspector," said the dean. The venerable archdeacon nodded, but said nothing.

Codlin's the friend, not Short, thought Littlejohn.

"Do you think it likely that, unknown to you, madam, and to you two gentlemen, the bishop might have got himself mixed up in something which endangered his life?"

Mrs. Macintosh shook her head, bewildered, and the two clerical escorts vigorously denied it.

"No, no, certainly not."

"Certainly not. No, no."

"But it is obvious someone was anxious to see him and even to do violence to him. Surely, he wouldn't have been called out at that time for a mere trifle . . . ."

"I am utterly at a loss . . . ."

"Did he seem distressed by the message? Or how did he seem, madam?"

"I should say rather excited. Not eagerly so, but . . . well . . . he tightened his lips, nodded to himself and got ready to go."

"Thank you. And now for a rather painful question, which I hesitate to put, but which might be very important . . . ."

Mrs. Macintosh opened her eyes wide and the two clerics leaned forward expectantly.

"The police surgeon found your husband's body in a very emaciated condition. So much so, that he said he looked famished. Can you explain that . . . ?"

The three of them looked at one another. The dean raised questioning eyebrows at Mrs. Macintosh and she nodded as though leaving the field to him.

"As one in his confidence, I may be able to explain, although the story is rather a strange one and might seem a little eccentric . . . ."

The archdeacon leaned back in his chair, sank lower in it, crossed his spindleshanks in their spotless gaiters and composed himself to show that he, too, knew what was coming.

"I doubt if you are aware, that the late bishop was also a qualified medical man. He was interested in psychiatry, which he hoped to link with spiritual healing. He had written books on the subject . . . ."

"Yes, sir. I am aware of that."

The dean looked surprised.

"You have heard? Of late, he has been engaged on a new book and new research. He and a psychiatrist of our town have been working together."

"Could you give me the name of the other doctor, please?"

"Dr. Mulroy, of Greyle . . . ."

Littlejohn noted it down in his book.

"Yes, sir?"

"The bishop was studying the mystic religions of the East. I am no expert on these matters and can only tell you what he mentioned to me in the course of discussing this new series of experiments. You may or may not be aware that developments in modern psychology deal with the deep unconscious and the relief from fear and tension by deep analysis. This is supposed to lead to a better way of life. Whether or not that is so, I cannot say, I am no expert . . . ."

"No," said the venerable archdeacon and the dean gave him an astonished look.

"In the East, however, certain practices, such as yoga, have long been in use and, I gather, have a close relationship with this deep unconscious and knowledge of it. So, you see, what our occidental scientists regard as new ground to be explored, has, by other routes, been already traversed by the mystics of the orient . . . ."

Everybody looked bewildered. The dean himself seemed a bit out of his depth and chose his words carefully.

Littlejohn was wondering what it all had to do with the bishop and his famished body.

" . . . Dr. Macintosh was experimenting in the oriental methods of contact with the deep unconscious."

The dean beamed as though it were all as plain as a pikestaff.

The archdeacon cleared his throat. He wasn't going to be left out of it, and plunged in at the deep-end.

"You see, Inspector, all these practices are extremely dangerous. In the hands of the inexpert and unwary they may result in the complete overthrow of the balance of the mind."

"You're not meaning to say, gentlemen, that the bishop's mind was unbalanced at the time of his death?"

"Certainly not," interposed Mrs. Macintosh and looked disgustedly at her two friends.

"I think what they are going to tell you is that my husband was experimenting in certain Eastern mystical practices which necessitated a measure of fasting for their success. In spite of my entreaties, he insisted in going on with them, limiting his meals to a mere minimum, and finally almost breaking down his health. That is why he had to take a holiday. He became very debilitated . . . ."

"I see. And were his experiments successful?"

"I think so, for the most part. He seemed pleased with them, although he never mentioned their nature fully."

The dean interrupted.

"I gathered they concerned the nature of halucinations and perhaps revelations arising from the state of fasting. Dr. Mulroy will know more than we do. He collaborated . . . ."

"I see. And do you think this . . . this series of experiments has anything to do with the case we now have in hand?"

"It is extremely unlikely."

"How long have you been staying here, Mrs. Macintosh?"

"Ten days, Inspector. We came for a month."

"And have you noticed anything whilst you've been here which seems connected with the crime?"

"I don't think so."

"Were you always together?"

"No, Inspector. My husband was a man who liked a measure of solitude in which even I did not share. He went for walks alone . . . ."

"Did he ever mention anything untoward or interesting which happened on such walks?"

"No. Except perhaps to remark on the pleasure they gave him, or the weather. But never of any encounters on the way."

"Was the bishop a wealthy man?"

"Not very. He rose from comparatively humble beginnings. He has saved, of course . . . ."

"You are the full beneficiary under his Will, I presume, madam?"

The two clergymen looked astonished at the impertinence, but Mrs. Macintosh didn't seem to mind.

"Yes, Inspector."

"Excuse the apparent curiosity and perhaps the liberty, but this is very important. Who is the beneficiary after you, Mrs. Macintosh?"

"The bishop's family, who live in Glebeshire. But as I have survived my husband, the estate is at my complete disposal . . . ."

There was a tap on the door and the hall-porter entered.

"Excuse me, madam, the maid has finished packing, the bags are down and the car is waiting . . . ."

"In that case, I'm sure you'll excuse us, Inspector," said Mrs. Macintosh. "Is there anything more?"

"No thank you, madam. I shall probably be in Greyle myself very soon and may take the liberty of calling on you there."

"Please do . . . ."

"And thank you all for your help and courtesy . . . ."

"Not at all . . . ."

The party filed out, Littlejohn making up the rear. They all shook hands with the Inspector, the archdeacon last.

"And I do hope you succeed in finding the perpetrator of this dreadful outrage quickly, Inspector," said the Venerable. "He was my best friend and I feel I owe it to him . . . ."

And with that he pattered off to join the others.

Chapter Seven
Cranage Farm

LITTLEJOHN wanted further background about the dead bishop so decided to go to Greyle to get it. Luckily the train passed within a few miles of Medhope, Macintosh's native place; the Inspector called there first.

Before he left Cape Mervin, he gave Cromwell full details of the crime to date and told him to keep his eyes and ears open both in the hotel and out of it. In particular, more information was required about the card players and Father O'Shaughnessy and his billiard playing friend.

Cromwell nodded gravely. It was like putting a good dog on the scent.

The train stopped at Perryton Junction and Littlejohn had to get a taxi for the remaining four miles. He was surprised when his decrepit conveyance stopped at Cranage Farm. It was hardly what he had expected.

Instead of a gracious black-and-white place, in keeping with most of the other farms in the neighbourhood, Cranage was a gaunt red-brick building with tall queer-shaped chimneys and misshapen wings jutting from the main block. A number of outbuildings joined by a high wall encircled the house, almost converting it into a small fortress. The place was spotlessly clean, but no amount of care could make the farm less sombre.

A dumpy maid with a limp answered the door. She had been weeping. News of the bishop's death had arrived there, for all the blinds were drawn, giving an even more ominous aspect to the existing gloom.

A tall, loose-limbed man followed almost on the heels of the maid. And a fair, stout woman came from another inner room at the same time.

It was as though a visitor to the front door was so rare that it brought out all the occupants of the house. Somewhere upstairs somebody was knocking impatiently with a stick on the floor.

The tall, dark man lost patience.

"It's all right, Emily," he said to the fair woman and at the same time dismissed the maid with an abrupt gesture. "It's the man from Scotland Yard Frank telephoned about. I'll see him. And tell mother to stop knocking. We can't do everything at once."

Littlejohn on the doorstep took it all in. Presumably Frank was Sir Francis and he had warned the family already of the police visit.

"Come in, Inspector. I'm the bishop's brother . . . ."

"Sir Francis Tennant has already told you I was coming, sir? I assume Frank is Sir Francis . . . ."

"Yes. He didn't want mother bothering. She's very old now and we don't like her disturbing. But come in . . . ."

When the front door was closed, you could hardly see a foot ahead of you. The dark corridor was heavy with pleasant smells. Ripe pears probably stored in the garrets, hay, and now and then, the scent of the dairy.

A shaft of bright daylight crossed the hall as Macintosh opened the door of one of the rooms. There was a hat-stand, a hall chair, a lot of coats hanging on pegs. Nothing more.

A staircase with a graceful mahogany handrail went up from one side.

The fair woman had gone upstairs and could be heard arguing with someone else. The other voice was sharp and quavering. Probably the old lady.

"You are not to go down, grannie. It'll only upset you. Now be good and stay in your chair . . . ."

"Come in here, Inspector."

The room was small and dark. A narrow sash window provided all the light, which seemed to fade out within a yard of it, leaving corners lost in gloom. A log fire burned in an old-fashioned grate. Even then, the place had a cold, damp smell. The furniture was out of date, too. A horsehair suite, two saddleback horsehair armchairs, a round mahogany table poised on a central claw-leg. There were little tables, too, crowded with souvenirs and knick-knacks. A family bible and photograph album on the heavy sideboard and a lot of old ornaments scattered about. The whole place was depressing.

Robert Macintosh had been writing. Pens, ink, paper and envelopes scattered on the table and a number of open letters as though he might have been answering them or seeking addresses from them. Probably dealing with correspondence arising out of his brother's death.

"You are not a farmer, sir?"

It was written all over him. He belonged to the professional type. Well-kept hands, good clothes, clean linen. And a sort of austerity about his movements. His face was like that of his dead brother; long, heavy, solemn. His features hardly moved, but you could see he was nervous. Perhaps the shock of the murder had put him off his balance.

"No. I'm a solicitor in practice in Medhope. My younger brother farms this place. He's about the buildings somewhere . . . . I am Robert; my brother is Rufus; and the bishop was James. Now you know us."

"I'm very sorry to bother you at a time like this, but immediate information is most important, sir, as you'll appreciate."

"Of course I do. Sit down. Now anything you wish to ask me . . . ."

"Thank you, sir."

The window faced a well-kept lawn bordered with fruit trees and with a large elm in the centre of it. Two horses were eating the leaves of the hawthorn hedge. Beyond stretched an endless succession of arable fields and pastures right to the skyline. Now and then you could hear faint explosions from distant quarries.

"This must have been a great shock to you all, sir . . . ."

"Yes. The murder of my brother has stunned us. It is quite unthinkable."

"You have no idea of what might have been the motive, I take it. I must confess it baffles us . . . ."

Robert Macintosh passed his large white hand over his bald forehead.

"What motive could there be? A bishop, a prominent and well-liked man, suddenly done to death with great violence. Incredible!"

"Do you know anything of your late brother's researches in psychology?"

The lawyer gave Littlejohn a sharp look. His hands were active all the time. He interlaced the fingers, tugged at them, fumbled with the seals on his watch-chain, dragged at his collar which seemed to choke him, pulled at his lower lip. Never still.

"So you know that already? No, I can't help you. My brother's medical researches were quite outside my orbit . . . ."

"You sound as if you didn't approve of them, all the same."

"I didn't. We rather got at cross-purposes about them. I think the clergy would do well to leave such things alone. They are the business of medical men . . . ."

"Your brother's zeal in that direction caused him to neglect his pastoral duties . . . ?"

"That too! You seem to know a lot, Inspector. But it was quite true. I feel it retarded his progress in the church."

"Do you think the work in any way unhinged your brother's mind? He was in a poor state of physical health when he died. His body was emaciated by experiments . . . ."

Robert Macintosh rose hastily to his feet and towered over Littlejohn.

"That state of my brother's mental health was perfect," he shouted in sudden anger.

He was livid. Then he recovered just as quickly.

"Pardon me, Inspector," he said quietly. "But that is a sore point with me. I saw him regularly and urged him to stop those devastating experiments, but he refused. The whole affair got on my nerves. To see his career jeopardised . . . ."

Macintosh shrugged his shoulders hopelessly.

"Were you here at the time of your brother's death, sir?" asked Littlejohn.

He gave the time and date.

Macintosh jerked himself upright.

"What is the purport of that question?" he asked in his best legal manner.

"Purely formal, as you are aware, sir."

"I was at a meeting of the Friends of Greyle Cathedral, a county body which raises funds for keeping good the structure of the building . . . . You can easily confirm that."

"Thank you, sir. And your brother Rufus?"

"At the farm, here, of course. You can hardly expect him to be elsewhere. These are busy days for farmers. He was hardly likely to be murdering his own brother sixty miles away at nearly midnight!"

Macintosh was growing heated again.

"I'm not suggesting any such thing, sir. We have these routine questions to ask . . . ."

"There are limits, Inspector."

Littlejohn was about to ask if he could see Rufus for a minute, when suddenly a great commotion broke out on the stairs.

"Now, mother, you know you mustn't . . . . Your heart . . . . Please be sensible . . . ."

"I *will* see him . . . ! I *will* see him . . . !"

Shuffling footsteps, the tapping of a stick, other footsteps hurrying upstairs and then, as the parties met, a further altercation.

"Stand aside, Esther! I order you . . . ! How dare you? Let me *go*. . . ."

Robert Macintosh rose and hurried across the room impatiently. Just in time to meet his mother in the doorway.

A furious, little old lady, red in the cheeks, her bluish lips puckered in petulant rage, her ebony stick gripped halfway, her body trembling. She had a round, wrinkled face and blue eyes flashing with anger.

"So *you're* the policeman! You don't look like one, I must say. Why waste time here when my son's blood calls for vengeance from far away? What has he done to deserve this? My dear son who grew up to be a bishop . . . ."

And then the rage which had sustained her suddenly ebbed. She sank on the settle by the door and began to weep noisily like a child.

"I told you, mother . . . "

The fair-haired woman fluttered helplessly about.

In the distance a violent explosion from the quarries . . . .

The old woman rocked herself to and fro and pettishly pushed away the hands of her daughter-in-law, who sought to get her to her feet.

"I said what it would be years ago when he married Evelyn. Ill-fated, it was, to have anything to do with Evelyn . . . ."

Robert Macintosh flapped his hands angrily.

"Be quiet, mother. Evelyn has nothing to do with this . . . ."

He filled a small glass with brandy and gave it to his mother.

"Drink it," he said fiercely. Then he turned almost craftily towards Littlejohn just to see how he was reacting to the disturbance.

"Now mother, go back to your room. You can do no good here and we'll tell you all about it later. You don't want to be ill again, do you?"

All the old lady's resistance was gone. She just sat and moaned to herself.

"I can't get back up the stairs, Robert. I can't. Let me stay, Robert. I'll be quiet. You, sir, you'll let me stay, won't you?"

She turned in childish, almost half-witted appeal to Littlejohn.

"I think you'd better be getting back to your room, madam. I'm going, you see. I'm so sorry you've been disturbed."

"I don't blame you, Mr . . . . Mr. who ever they call you. But I want to hear what they're saying about my son . . . my dead son. I'm his mother . . . I've a right to hear . . . ."

Hob-nailed boots sounded in the passage and the doorway was filled by the huge frame of Rufus Macintosh. His name suited him. He had red hair, red face and a red moustache. Quite unlike the other members of the family. Huge, simple, homely type, with probably a hot temper. He had a shaggy old sheepdog at his heels.

"Why mother! What are you doing down here?"

The old lady stretched out her arms to Rufus like a frightened child.

"I came down and I can't get back. Robert says I'm to go back, but nobody cares how I get back, Rufus."

"What's the meaning of this, Robert? Can't you see she's all in?"

Rufus's temper was rising.

"Come, mother . . . ."

He picked her up like a bundle of feathers and, with her arms round his neck, gently carried her off and upstairs.

"And now, Robert . . . "

Rufus was down again and was mad with his brother. The veins of his forehead stood out swollen and livid. His mother must have been telling him her troubles . . . .

A hot-tempered, cross-grained lot, thought Littlejohn.

Robert had opened his mouth to tell his tale, when suddenly there was a further commotion. This time it sounded to come from high up in the garrets.

The voice of Emily, the lame maid, was heard in a high-pitched shout.

"Mr. Robert! Mr. Robert! Mr. Rufus . . . ! Miss Barbara's out of her room and I can't get her back. She's coming down . . . Mr. Rufus!"

Both brothers made for the door and rushed up the stairs, jostling and impeding each other in their hurry. Their heavy, eager feet made the whole staircase rock.

Then, from above came a series of piercing shrieks followed by peal upon peal of demoniacal laughter.

The sheep-dog leapt from the hearth, turned his muzzle to the ceiling and howled dismally.

Littlejohn was left alone and unheeded.

Chapter Eight
Official Help

THE day was fine and warm and Littlejohn had paid-off his taxi intending to walk the three miles back to the station.

The commotion at Cranage Farm made him keener than ever to stroll on his own and think out the whole confused business.

His visit to Cranage had been a complete fiasco, yielding no fruit except a picture of a very strange family and a mixed lot of alibis.

A rare old, fair old rickety-rackety crew!

First, the bishop himself. Emaciated, neglecting his work and probably his wife in the pursuit of what might be esoteric knowledge. An eccentric in fact, with a mistaken sense of proportion concerning his pastoral duties. A promising career, as likely as not cut short by an outbreak of a family taint . . . .

Then his brother, Robert, a large man with the face of a pious burglar. Nervy, irritable, and apparently the dominating force of the Macintosh family.

Rufus, the other, red, slow-moving, slow-thinking.

Mrs. Macintosh, the mother, senile, childish, half-demented.

And, finally, Barbara, the sister, evidently quite off her head. Altogether confined to her room among the attics.

There must be some strain of inherited mental weakness in the family and this had even extended to the dead bishop himself.

Robert Macintosh, after quietly and firmly getting his sister to her room, with many cries and lamentations on her part, had returned to Littlejohn, and begged him to go and come back at a more suitable time.

"My sister is suffering from nervous breakdown and has just been gravely disturbed by hearing from Emily, a most stupid woman, that my brother is dead. I shall be needed upstairs again in a minute or so. So, if you don't mind . . . ."

What could one do?

Littlejohn had departed after arranging to call again in the near future.

He smoked his pipe as he strode along. There was something very comforting in tobacco. After the ominous strain of Cranage it reminded one of the saner things in life.

All the same, he must get to know something about the strange Macintosh family as soon as possible. There must be somebody who could tell the inside story.

The *somebody* quickly materialised like the genie of the lamp.

Littlejohn was approaching cross-roads and suddenly, sailing along the hedge of the by-road at right angles to the one along which the Inspector was walking, appeared a large red face under a regulation helmet. The mouth was opening and closing slowly and mournfully.

Oh, Genevieve, sweet Genevieve,

The days may come, the days may go . . . .

At the cross-roads, the head suddenly took to itself a large corpulent body, mounted on a bicycle, with long rotating legs and enormous boots propelling it.

A policeman like a huge blowfly soared into view, still singing in a loud untrained bass, with now and then a flat instead of a natural breaking into his song.

The singing ceased in the middle of a bar as the bobby spotted Littlejohn. He cleared his throat, turned red, looked sheepish, and said good morning.

"Good morning, constable. The very man!"

The policeman seemed instinctively to scent a superior officer. He braked, wobbled and then nimbly leapt from his bike.

"Yes, sir."

He eyed Littlejohn wondering whether it was murder, arson or lost watches and fountain-pens. It was always watches and fountain-pens. Or else dogs! Never anything exciting.

"I'm Detective-Inspector Littlejohn of Scotland Yard . . . ."

The bobby almost let fall his bike. He was holding it with his right hand and executed a grotesque movement to release himself for a smart salute which he delivered with some difficulty.

"Constable Prickwillow, sir, at your service."

At your service. That was good. Prickwillow determined to remember that bit when he reported to his wife later in the day.

"Say it again, constable . . . ."

The large, red-moustached face broke into a cheerful grin. The constable was a merry man at heart. He prided himself on a sense of humour and here he recognised a kindred spirit.

"Prickwillow, sir. Quite a common name in the parts I come from . . . ."

"I see. It's a new one to me."

Littlejohn produced his warrant-card and the policeman gravely perused it, his lips moving as he read, and then he handed it back.

"Let's sit on this gate and have a talk, Prickwillow. I'm needing some help and you've arrived at just the right time."

The bobby carefully parked his shining bicycle, hoisted himself on the top bar of the gate and Littlejohn followed suit. The Inspector passed his cigarette-case, but Prickwillow hesitated. He was on duty and therefore cautious. He had a nice little house and a comfortable job. He wasn't going to . . .

Eventually, he was persuaded. The cigarette looked queer under the large brown moustache. Like a little lighthouse in a wild sea.

"Where are you stationed, constable?"

"Medhope village, sir. Mile and a half back along the road I come along."

"Do you know the Macintoshes of Cranage?"

The bobby removed his cigarette carefully between a huge thumb and index and flicked off the ash with his little finger.

"Yes, sir. Know 'em well. Known 'em since I was a boy . . . ."

"You know Bishop Macintosh of Greyle, then. He's just been murdered."

"Yes, sir. Very sad affair. Family had a lot of trouble lately. A queer lot . . . ."

A drove of hedge flies began to buzz and circle round Prickwillow's honest, sweating face and he flailed them off and started to puff furiously at his cigarette to gas them.

"What sort of trouble?"

"Well . . . Young Barbara's been as mad as an 'atter for years. A love affair, they say. And the old lady's broken down under the strain. Used to be a proper old dragon, did Mrs. Macintosh. Ran the farm *and* the family. Like a proper sergeant-major. Now, they say, she spends most of the day countin' her fingers. Sad. Very sad."

Prickwillow looked heartbroken.

"Did you know the Bishop of Greyle, Prickwillow?"

"Yes, sir, I did. Man and boy I've been in these parts for forty-eight years come Martinmass and I reckon I've seen most people grow up round here."

"What did you think of the bishop?"

"A very nice gentleman indeed. Very affable. Always a pleasant word for people, but a bit grim, like . . . ."

"Grim?"

"Well . . . No sense o' humour. Very civil, but never a one for a joke. Now the local vicar here . . . He's another cup of tea altogether. Proper caution . . . ."

"Yes, but what about the bishop?"

"You might call the Macintoshes a grim family. A grim history, too."

"Go on . . . ."

The constable extinguished the cigarette, which was now singeing his moustache, by rubbing it against the gatepost, blew through his whiskers and looked at a loss for words.

"Well, sir . . . It's a bit awkward to explain. A queer sort o' family. Cranage has a peculiar atmosphere. Personally, I'm not surprised at anybody goin' potty there. That house!"

"What's wrong with it?"

"Isolated, you know. And some houses are just queer. No describing 'em in detail, sir. They're just queer, that's all there is to it."

"Has the farm a bad history?"

"Well . . . yes. Now my missus, who's a bit of a reader, sir . . . always gets two books a week out o' the County Library . . . *and* not just slop or thrillers but good books . . . my missus always calls Cranage *Wuthering Heights.* A bit literary, eh?"

The bobby looked at Littlejohn's face trying to sum-up the Inspector's judgment of his wife's intelligence.

"She reads the Brontës, does she? She's evidently got good taste."

"Yes, sir, she 'as. I don't do much readin' myself, sir. Kept pretty busy in my garden and on duty. But one night, my missus reads me a passage from that book, *Wutherin' Heights,* I mean. She reads in bed a lot, you see. Well, with just a bedside lamp on and dark all round the rest o' the room, what she read gave me quite a turn. Just hit off Cranage to a T, it did. Put me in such a mood, that I had to get up and take a look at the kids sleepin' in the next room and pat the dog as he lay on the hearthrug just to sort o' restore me good humour with the ordinary, 'appy things of life, as you may say . . . ."

"But about the history of the place. What about that?"

"Well . . . I'm not exactly a scholar. You ought to ask the vicar about that. The farmhouse has been there for about three hundred years and there's always been funny goings on. The Macintoshes have been tenants for near on a hundred years themselves. One of 'em's committed suicide, another's gone off her head, and now one's been murdered. If things go on like this the place ought to be burned to the ground before worse 'appens . . . ."

Here the constable made a sweeping, destructive gesture with his hand and arm and almost overbalanced and fell off his perch.

"They say that two brothers who built the farm quarrelled about religion and ruined themselves in a sort of competition as to who could build himself the finest church. If you're staying in these parts you'll find those two churches at Storton and Hallby . . . ."

"But what about the Macintoshes?"

"The husband of the present old lady committed suicide when quite young and left her to bring up the family. Nobody quite knew why he did it. There was talk of one of the maidservants and him . . . . But Mrs. Macintosh soon put that down. On the other hand, the old folk do say there is definite insanity in the family. It doesn't take much to drive them off their rockers, as you might say."

"What about Miss Barbara?"

"I was comin' to that . . . . A love affair, they say."

"Any details?"

"A most unfortunate one, I must say. You see, Bishop Macintosh married a Miss Evelyn Creer, member of a local landed family. A love match, they say. She was a very lovely girl and half the county was after her. Everybody was staggered when they announced their wedding, including both families. The bishop was just a plain reverend then and vicar of somewhere or other. His family said she'd do *him* no good and her family said he'd do *her* no good."

"And Miss Barbara?"

"I'm comin' to that. Miss Evelyn had a younger brother, a bit of a rip, and he got sweet on Miss Barbara. They got engaged, too. This time *his* family was pleased. Thought it 'ud stop him wenching all over the countryside. But '*er* family played merry hell again. What with the bishop and his sister, Cranage must have been a bedlam at the time."

"And what happened?"

"Well . . . Apparently, Mr. Rupert, that's Miss Evelyn's brother, couldn't be content with Miss Barbara, but must go and give one of the village girls a baby between gettin' engaged and married. Well . . . the marriage didn't come off. Mr. Rufus Macintosh went over to see Mr. Rupert with a huntin' crop and half killed him. Rupert cleared off to South Africa or somewhere and between them they just messed up

Miss Barbara's life properly. She went right off her head and has been that way for more than a dozen years."

"And they keep her locked up at Cranage?"

"They do, sir. And it's a damned shame. She might have been cured if they'd sent her to a proper place for those sort of folks. But no, the Macintoshes don't work that way. They have to be different."

"You don't sound to like the Macintoshes, Prickwillow."

"I don't, sir. I don't like 'em at all. I never had any personal trouble myself with them, but I've had a devil of a time keeping them *out* of trouble. Settin' the dogs on tramps, or even firing guns at intruders. I know you don't want all the scum of the roads and countryside hangin' around your place, but there are limits as to 'ow you treat 'em . . . ."

"I agree. And was the bishop a frequent visitor at Cranage?"

"Yes, sir. Miss Barbara was his favourite sister. He was very put out about the scandal. He and Miss Evelyn were married before it happened, otherwise, it might have been off between them, too. As it is, old Mrs. Macintosh won't have the bishop's wife near the place. So the bishop had to visit them by himself. He was very concerned about his sister's condition and tried all ways to help her . . . ."

"Yes, he was a doctor, too, I gather, and interested in things of the mind."

"That's right, sir. Not that I agree with that sort o' thing. What do the clergy want messing about with medicine for? Why can't they leave it to the doctors? It's the doctors' bread and butter, sir. I don't hold with . . . "

"Well, Prickwillow, I'd be very grateful if you'd just keep an eye on Cranage for a while and let me know if anything unusual occurs there."

"Such as . . . sir?"

"Well . . . Strange visitors, say, or unusual comings and goings. This murder might cause a lot of upset there. Will you do that?"

"Certainly, sir. I'll converge my patrols to include the roads round there and keep my eyes open . . . ."

Littlejohn gave Prickwillow his card.

"News addressed to Scotland Yard will be forwarded to me."

They let themselves down from the gate and Prickwillow gathered up his bicycle.

"Good day, sir . . . ."

In the distance a train whistled.

"That's your train, sir, leaving Hallby. You've just nice time. Ten minutes . . . ."

They parted with a handshake and Prickwillow, after a brisk salute, mounted his bicycle. He started to hum to himself almost as soon as the pedals began to turn and as though his energy increased with his velocity, burst into song almost before he was out of Littlejohn's hearing.

And whether we part or meet,
I shall love you the same for ever,
As . . . long . . . as . . . my hearrrrrt shall beat.

Chapter Nine
The Sniper

ON the way to the station Littlejohn changed his mind about the train.

The constable had mentioned the vicar as being well-versed in local history. Perhaps he could tell him more about the Macintosh and Creer families and the tragic romances which had agitated them.

A church spire rose from among a clump of trees about a mile away. The vicarage wouldn't be far from that.

Littlejohn was walking briskly along the highway to the distant station. To the right, a by-road suddenly branched off, marked by a rough signpost.

"To Perryton Station, 1 mile, 6 furlongs."

"To Medhope, 1 mile."

The latter pointing to the secondary road.

Littlejohn turned sharply to the right and took the way to Medhope.

It was very pleasant and pretty. From the highroad, with thick hawthorn hedges flanking and hiding the flat fields on either side, to an open, fenced track, which finally cut its way through a small forest.

Tall beech trees on either side of the road. Deep undergrowth and shadow beneath the trees and bushes of the forest and the foliage almost meeting over the road and forming a dark, green tunnel.

A cock pheasant strutted across and vanished in the cover. On the macadam the carcases of two small rabbits, completely flattened by a passing car, probably the night before.

Littlejohn enjoying his stroll, strode through the dim tunnel of leaves. At the far end the light thinned, revealing, framed in the distance, more open country and a farmhouse and buildings, with conical haystacks and a dutch barn. In the far distance, Medhope church tower again.

There seemed to be thunder in the air. Hardly a leaf stirred and the birds were still and quiet. Somewhere beyond the woods cows began to moo, for it was nearing milking time.

The Inspector, interested in the wild life after seeing the pheasant, slackened speed as he walked through the cutting. He took off his hat and mopped his hot forehead. Now and then a gate gave access to the spinney. Broken bottles, wood-ash and rusty tins revealed the presence of past picnickers, campers, and tramps.

He had his eyes on Medhope weathercock, a crooked object on a pole on top of the church tower, when it happened.

At first, Littlejohn thought it was a flying beetle. It passed his ear with a swift, singing noise. But almost at once he realised it was travelling too fast for an insect. It was a bullet!

Hastily he turned in his tracks. He had passed the forest and was in the open again. On each side flat fields, mostly arable, fenced with posts and wire. There was no sign of life at all in the spinney behind.

On the spur of the moment, the Inspector retraced his steps to the wood, walking sharply at first, then trotting. He had an idea he might come upon whoever had fired the shot in the forest and tell him off for dangerous shooting so near the highway. Or he might drive him into the open and perhaps recognise him.

It might have been an accident. Or it might . . .

Then . . .

A flash of flame leapt from the middle of a bramble bush. There was a sharp crack. But before the explosion a jerk in the fleshy part of Littlejohn's thigh. No other sound from the forest.

Littlejohn was down in the road. His leg gave way under him and from a hole in his trouser leg blood began to gush rhythmically. Every pulse brought a fresh spurt.

He looked round. Not a soul about. Sweat poured from him, bathed his head and ran down over his face and behind his ears. His underclothing was soon wet through.

He fumbled with his leg, located the wound and jabbed it with a handkerchief which at once became soaked in blood. The cloth of his trousers was sticky with it. He tried to get to his feet again, but the wounded limb was numb.

Littlejohn cursed. He'd have to make a tourniquet quickly, or he'd faint from loss of blood and perhaps bleed to death, for he was bleeding at an alarming rate. He hadn't much pain, but strength seemed to ebb from his very marrow with every beat of his heart.

A silly predicament! Weakening from loss of blood in broad daylight within hailing distance of a farm!

The Inspector took a silk handkerchief from his breast pocket, knotted it above the wound and sought for something to use as a tourniquet. He hadn't brought his walking stick and all he could find was a pencil, almost too short. It snapped in two as he turned it. Then, he remembered his pipe and used it, screwing the handkerchief until the blood ceased to flow, leaving the limb feeling cold and dead.

As he swayed his body upright, two more sharp cracks sounded almost simultaneously with dull thuds in the road a few inches from where he was squatting. Little clouds of dust rose. The man with the rifle was firing again.

Littlejohn flattened his body in the dust and grit and began to shout at the top of his voice.

"Help!"

It sounded silly. Like play-acting at a rehearsal. A broken, feeble, almost false cry. He didn't seem to have any breath left for the effort and his voice was hoarse and spent. He found his police-whistle and blew it. It was a broken-winded effort.

It was just nonsense. A large, able-bodied man, fit for anything, suddenly reduced to dangerous impotence by a small hole in the leg. And providing a sitting target for some sniper hidden in the woods.

Littlejohn tried to creep to the farm, but failed. He painfully dragged himself along keeping splayed in the road as best he could.

He wondered vaguely who had fired the shot. Was he still watching and preparing to break cover and finish him off by a nearer effort? It didn't really matter. All he cared about was getting to the farm. All his energy became focussed on that.

The posts by the roadside grew blurred and dimly duplicated. Like when your spectacles don't synchronise and give you two uncertain images. And the sun was shining brightly, yet darkness seemed to be falling.

Surely, he wasn't going to faint! He'd been coshed into unconsciousness and knocked out by fists a time or two, but he'd never fainted before. But that was what happened. It came all at once and he remembered nothing more.

From the farm emerged a shambling, unkempt cowman. His eyes were fixed on the distant fields where the cows were grazing and waiting for milking.

"Cooop, coooop . . . cawm on," he yelled shrilly.

The cows raised their heads, listened calmly and then began slowly to move through the open gates to where the man was standing.

Then he saw Littlejohn. He didn't increase his speed, but ambled to the unconscious form as though the sight of it were an everyday event. He was still calling the cows.

He didn't even touch Littlejohn. His intelligence didn't seem to grasp the situation at all. He pushed his greasy, cow-hair covered cap to the back of his bullet head and scratched his poll. He thought a bit and then turned to the farm and yelled : "Luke! . . . Oi! . . . Luke!" as though still calling home the cattle.

Littlejohn became aware of thick eyebrows, then two kindly eyes, a short moustache and a handsome brown face.

"Hullo! We're getting you to the cottage hospital. The doctor wasn't in, so we 'phoned there. They said to bring you . . . . Feeling better?"

A fresh young fellow, who looked like a farmer's son. Clean and fair and healthy-looking. He was squatting on the floor of the vehicle looking anxiously at the Inspector.

There was a bandage round Littlejohn's leg with a round ebony ruler where the pipe had been. They'd slit the trouser leg from top to bottom.

"Drink this . . . ."

The acrid tang of brandy and a burning pain in his gullet. Littlejohn felt a bit brighter and smiled at his friend.

"Thanks. Sorry to be such a bother . . . ."

"You were all-in when we found you. What happened?"

"I seem to have stopped a stray shot . . . ."

Littlejohn didn't feel up to giving full explanations. Besides, it didn't seem policy to do so. After all, he didn't know who the young man was.

"We've let the police know . . . ."

"Prickwillow?"

"Yes. He'll meet us at the hospital. You know him?"

"Good! Yes, I've met him . . . ."

A land girl was driving the car, a shooting-brake. They'd laid him on a mattress on the floor with a cushion under his head. The road was bad and the van bumped over the pot-holes. The girl, in trying to avoid them, swayed the vehicle from side to side. It made Littlejohn feel sick . . . .

Things happened as in a drunken stupor.

The bumping and gliding of the truck. Then, brakes being gently applied. The bright sunshine as they opened the doors of the van. Two men with a stretcher which they placed on a trolley. A swing door. "Easy, easy . . . ." A little fat middle-aged matron in a grey uniform and apron and a younger nurse in a washed-out purple dress.

"Straight to the theatre . . . ."

The easy gliding of the trolley, the smell of antiseptics.

"Here's Dr. Simpson . . . ."

"Let's have a look at you . . . ."

The young surgeon in his singlet and trousers washing his hands. Interminably soaping . . . .

The sharp prick of a hypodermic.

Nothing more.

Chapter Ten
The Cottage Hospital

ALL the images were confused and blurred at first, but slowly came into focus. A moustache, then two anxious eyes, and finally the solid form of Prickwillow standing by a nurse. The nurse nodded and she and Prickwillow looked pleased and relieved.

"Ahem!" said Prickwillow and covered his mouth with his hand. He looked ready to make a speech of welcome.

"You can have a word with him now, but the doctor says he's not to be worried or tired . . . ."

"Feelin' better now, sir?"

"Not much . . . . Give me time . . . ."

Littlejohn was beginning to remember things. The shot, the crawl to the farm. The journey in the cart.

"Feel well enough to tell me what happened, sir?"

Littlejohn felt sick inside. There seemed so much talking to do and so little energy with which to get it off his chest . . . .

"What time is it, Prickwillow?"

"Five o'clock . . . ."

So, it was three or four hours since it happened. The sharp-shooter must have got clean away long ago. Littlejohn remembered he hadn't had any lunch either. Funny that should strike him as important . . . .

"Always somebody shootin' too near the road, sir. A near go, if I may say so . . . ."

"This was deliberate, Prickwillow. Somebody tried to pot me off."

"What!"

Prickwillow jerked himself up hastily and ran from the foot of the bed to Littlejohn's side as though trying to shield him with his own body against anyone who might try another shot.

"You don't mean to say . . . "

"I do. Lucky for me somebody couldn't shoot straight. I got it in the leg instead of the head. And having winged me and finding me moving, he shot at me again . . . Twice, I think. Oh yes, it was deliberate."

"But who could it have been, sir?"

Littlejohn felt tired and irritable.

"Don't ask me, man. I don't know. But I want you to have the woods searched to see what can be found. Not that there's much to find. The shot was fired from the right-hand side of the road coming from where you and I parted company. I suppose the doctor's extracted the bullet. What was it?"

"A point four-four, sir. Rifle bullet . . . ."

Prickwillow was completely flabbergasted. He remained rooted to the spot, playing with the helmet in his hand and staring at Littlejohn's face like somebody in a trance.

"Has anybody been advised of this . . . accident?"

"No, sir. You see I didn't . . . "

Littlejohn groaned. There seemed such a lot to do. He wanted just to shut his eyes and fade out into the swimming air around him. He was quite light headed and felt he didn't care a damn what happened so long as they'd leave him alone.

"Telephone Cape Mervin police station. Tell them I've had an accident and to let my wife know, but not to alarm her. And to tell Sergeant Cromwell, who's there, to come at once. Even if he has to travel by taxi . . . . Get here with all speed. And bring Letty . . . my wife . . . with him . . . ."

"What about me, sir? Can I do anythin' in the way of . . . "

"I can't think what . . . "

Prickwillow receded into mists and the last he heard was the nurse's voice.

"That's enough. He's exhausted. No wonder, the blood he lost . . . . The road was swimming they said . . . . Tomorrow . . . "

Next morning he felt better. Cromwell and Mrs. Littlejohn had arrived the previous night and found him asleep, so had gone to stay at the village inn.

Littlejohn was propped up in bed, had eaten a light breakfast and felt in shape for more talk. The sun was shining through the windows and outside you could hear children passing to school and farm carts and cars trundling along the highway. There must have been a blacksmith's shop handy, too, for Littlejohn found himself imagining what was going on from the sounds. The gentle triplets as the smith tapped the anvil with his hammer and then the muffled ringing strokes on hot iron . . . .

Cromwell arrived. He had a vivid red weal across his forehead where his bowler hat had bitten, and he looked very annoyed. Letty was with him, but Cromwell didn't leave the pair together for exchange of any personal endearments or whatever they might want to say. Somebody had tried to shoot Littlejohn and that was priority number one!

Letty had been talking to the doctor. She wanted to take Littlejohn back with her either home or to Cape Mervin. Littlejohn insisted on the latter. The doctor said he could be moved by ambulance the following day, so Mrs. Littlejohn had fixed it all up at their hotel.

"But who . . . ? Why . . . ?" said Cromwell.

"Somebody thinks I know more than I do. It's evident I was followed. Maybe it was all the way from Cape Mervin. Or it might be one of the Cranage lot . . . ."

And he told Cromwell the result of his visits to Cranage and his talk with Prickwillow.

"Where is Prickwillow, by the way?"

"He's been in and out of here like a jack-in-the-box since we arrived. He's rustled up two more policemen from the county force and they've been combing the woods. Not a thing found. Whoever did it must even have carted away his empty rifle cartridges."

"I didn't expect they'd find anything. At any rate, we'd better fix a definite plan of campaign. I'm *hors de combat* for a while, but I'd still like to direct operations from my bed . . . . Unless The Yard insist on sending somebody else, can you manage and keep me posted?"

"Yes. Of course. I suppose I'd better stay at this end. Better clear up the shooting, hadn't we? It might lead us in the right direction . . . ."

"I'm sure it will. I'll fix up with Bowater for somebody to be legs and eyes for me in the town and try to work the thing out from bed. It all depends on whether Bowater cottons-on to the idea."

"Well, what had I better do first here?"

"Check up on the Cranage lot to start with. Find out where they all were at the time I was shot . . . . About one o'clock yesterday. And also get to know as much about the Macintosh family as you can. There's a local family called Creer, too. They're at cross-purposes with the Macintoshes, although the bishop's wife is one of the Creers. Go into their history, will you, and trace, if you can, what happened to Rupert Creer who seems to have gone abroad? Prickwillow will be a great help there, I should think."

"Weren't you on your way to Greyle, though? Ought we to pursue some enquiries there, as well?"

"Yes. I wanted to know exactly what was the nature of the work the bishop was doing with Dr. Mulroy and what Mulroy thought of him. We've not a ghost of an idea what the motive of the crime might have been and mustn't leave a stone unturned."

"Right. I'll take on where you left off, though. I'd like a few minutes alone with the chap that fired that shot . . . ."

"So would I . . . ."

The vicar had called. The nurse didn't know whether or not Littlejohn wanted to see him. The Inspector remembered that was exactly what he had been going to do when the sniper put paid to him.

"Oh, yes. Show him in, please. Good of him to call . . . ."

"You're on fire!"

The vicar had put his lighted pipe in his pocket as he entered the hospital and had set fire to his handkerchief. There was quite a commotion and a smell of burning before they got him settled.

"Forgive me . . . . I'm always doing it. I'm so sorry this has happened, Inspector Johnson . . . ."

"Littlejohn . . . ."

"I beg your pardon. They told me Johnson. Now I wonder why they did that? I must apologise for the accident in my parish. Those boys *will* shoot rooks too near the road. I shall speak to Prickwillow about it. I hope you are much improved."

He was small and portly with a ruddy countryman's complexion. His features were very mobile as though made from indiarubber and he kept screwing them up in a nervous spasm which so altered them that he momentarily looked like quite another man. His name was The Reverend the Honorable Thomas Gomm. The parishioners said the three bells in the steeple said "Hang Tom Gomm . . . ." That showed their affection for him. He had been Christening, marrying and burying them for forty-three years.

Littlejohn said hang him, too, after the vicar had called him Inspector Johnson about a dozen times. It so got on Cromwell's nerves that he had to take a turn in the garden whilst the two men talked. The thought that anyone shouldn't know Littlejohn in the first place was quite enough; to give him another name, was the limit!

It would be extremely tedious to give verbatim all that passed between Littlejohn and the Rev. the Hon. Tom Gomm. The old gentleman's memory was failing and events quite irrelevant to the point in hand kept leaking into his tale.

He knew all about the Creers. William Creer, Peter Creer, Joseph Creer. Old Uncle Tom Creer and all. He kept rhyming off their eccentricities. A queer wild family . . . .

Littlejohn almost fainted from weakness; it got so much on his nerves.

Finally, Rupert Creer.

"I remember Rupert well, Inspector Johnson. A weak good-looking boy. Or . . . was that Arthur? I can't be sure. But I do know Rupert got a village girl into trouble just before I put up the banns for him and Barbara Macintosh. Poor girl. It drove her quite off her head. And the Macintosh family were so vindictive that Rupert had to go off to South Africa . . . or was it Kenya? No. South Africa. Because I remember we were at war with them when I was curate at St. Ninian's Roseley. Just my little system of mnemonics, Inspector Johnson. Very useful . . . ."

"Could you tell me when all this occurred, sir?"

"Let me see. It was the year of the great blight. Blight . . . light . . . Lead Kindly Light . . . Hymn 193 . . . Nineteen thirty something. A little system I have, Inspector . . . ."

"Can you be a bit more precise?"

"I'm afraid . . . "

The vicar stroked his chin gently. It was very flexible and looked ready to come away in his hand.

"The illegitimate child would be Christened, no doubt, sir . . . ."

"Oh, yes, yes, yes. Without a doubt."

"What was the mother's name?"

"Forty."

"I beg pardon . . . ."

"Mary Forty. The postman's daughter, she was. She married the blacksmith later and he took the child as his own."

"We could check the dates of all these happenings from the church registers then, sir?"

"Yes . . . I'll do it with pleasure."

Littlejohn could imagine The Hon. Tom Gomm hunting through his registers at the rate he was at present dispensing information!

"I'll ask my assistant, Cromwell, to give you a hand, vicar."

"Cromwell, did you say, Inspector Johnson? How very interesting. I shall remember that easily. Marston Moor."

"My name's Littlejohn, by the way, not Johnson . . . ."

"To be sure. How stupid of me. I shall remember it in future. The diminutive . . . . Yes, yes . . . ."

"Was Mister Rupert heard of much after he left, sir? Had he any friends or his family with whom he kept in touch . . . ?"

"I really couldn't say. But I think he was what is know as a remittance man and perhaps the local bank would know if they sent him money."

"A very good idea, vicar. There is a local bank, then?"

"Yes. The London and South Counties have a sub-office here which opens Wednesdays and Fridays. Most people round about bank there. All the Easter offering cheques are on them . . . ."

"In that case, I'll send out some enquiries."

"Yes. A very helpful man is Tiplady, the clerk-in-charge. Most helpful. I remember once losing a cheque . . . ."

The Rev. the Hon. Tom Gomm prattled on. To Littlejohn his tubby outline slowly became like jelly and mist, the room darkened, and the Inspector slid into unconsciousness from sheer exhaustion.

" . . . You will do well to see Tiplady, Inspector Littlejohnson. I . . . Well, I never!"

Tom Gomm looked hard at Littlejohn and listened to his steady breathing. The Inspector was fast asleep. The vicar cocked an ear. Not a sound, except a bee buzzing in the window and some farm carts passing. The room was so cool and peaceful. Different from the hot village street at this stifling hour. Mr. Gomm eyed the easy chair with its foot rests and well-sprung seat. Why not? After all, it was a form of pastoral duty. Watching by the sick. He sank in the chair with a sigh, folded his neat little hands across his neat little paunch and closed his eyes . . . .

When Cromwell returned The Rev. and Hon. and his friend Inspector Littlejohnson were snoring harmoniously . . . .

Chapter Eleven
The Remittance Man

THEY took Littlejohn back to Port Mervin in an ambulance. He got a bit impatient at all the commotion. After two days at the cottage hospital, waited on hand and foot and fed like a fighting-cock, he felt ready to walk miles. But the doctor was strict about it.

"You'd feel different if you tried to get out of bed. Another two or three days rest then you can try a little walk . . . ."

The Inspector was fed up.

They put him back in his own room at the hotel, but moved the bed to the window so that he could see what was going on outside. He could look down on the drive of the hotel and watch the guests going out after meals and returning hungrily after their excursions. Shipping, too, came and went in the harbour and up the river. Anything from pleasure boats and fishing vessels to fairly large coasters. Each new arrival heralded by blasts on the siren and tiny figures on the rostrum outside the harbourmaster's office, gesticulating and showing the officers where to go and where to moor. Beyond, a vast stretch of sea with a cloud-flecked sky meeting it.

Littlejohn spent a lot of time gazing vacantly at the line where sea and sky met and turning over in his mind the facts of the queer case on which he was engaged.

It seemed to divide itself into two parts.

One thing was certain. The crime was deliberate and carefully planned. But who had done it? Someone from Greyle or the bishop's native place? Or had Macintosh stumbled into a hornets' nest in Mervin and paid dearly for his interference? And had whoever took pot-shots at Littlejohn followed him from Port Mervin or been stimulated to attempted murder by his appearance at Cranage?

He pondered idly. Mrs. Littlejohn was sitting in the room with him knitting him a pair of socks from coupon-free wool. Visitors were winding their ways home to the hotel and below, through the open windows of the dining-room, you could hear the waitresses laying the tables for lunch and rattling pots and cutlery.

"What's Cromwell doing? He ought to be here by now . . . ."

"Give him a chance. His train's not due in Mervin till one o'clock and it's not a quarter-to yet . . . ."

"Sorry. I'm getting a bit fed-up with this inactivity. Time's precious . . . ."

Mrs. Littlejohn was counting stitches and didn't reply.

Then Superintendent Bowater arrived. He seemed to fill the room with his huge bulk. He was full of solicitude for Littlejohn, indignation at the attempt on the Inspector's life, and anxiety concerning the case at his end.

"I wish you'd never dragged him into this," said Mrs. Littlejohn. "He wasn't too good when we came here for a rest. Now, he's worse and worrying himself to death because he can't get up and run about after clues . . . ."

Bowater had no sense of humour and didn't know what to say in reply.

"I . . . I . . . "

"Never mind, Superintendent," said Littlejohn. "Tell me, can it be possible that the bishop stumbled across something shady in the neighbourhood and paid for his curiosity with his life?"

Bowater looked abashed. The thought of shady goings-on in his district filled him with dismay.

"What do you mean by shady?"

"Well . . . Let's say some racket or other. Extensive black-market . . . ."

"Black-market? I know it does go on. Some of the local farmers . . . ."

"No, no, no. Bigger than that. Robberies to feed the market."

"None that I know of. And if there'd been any, we'd have known, wouldn't we?"

"What about smuggling? This is a port and very convenient for Eire . . . *and* the Continent at a pinch."

"Yes. We've been warned to be on the look-out. Same with the Customs Officers. Tobacco, silk, drinks and the like. But, so far, we've come across very little. The customs have tapped the men on some of the coasters. But, you see, there's little passenger traffic here."

"I don't mean that, Bowater. I mean a regular system of contraband running. Some of the local vessels working for a syndicate."

Bowater laughed heavily.

"O, come, Inspector. There's nothing of the kind here. And if there were, how would the reverend gentleman come to be mixed up in it?"

He looked pityingly at Littlejohn as though suspecting that his wound had affected his mind.

"Well, Superintendent, you might question your men and ask them to keep their eyes open. This is a bit of a remote place and I'd think there are a few quiet spots for a bit of smuggling . . . ."

Bowater shrugged his shoulders and spread out his huge fingers like ten sausages.

"Of course, if you think it'll do any good. Anything to help. Have as many men as you like, sir. Anything more I can do . . . ?"

There the conversation ended for Dr. Tordopp entered. He was attending Littlejohn.

"Hullo, doctor," said Bowater.

Tordopp gave him a curt greeting. Hostilities looked ready to break out again between the two men.

To prevent himself smiling Littlejohn began to count the roses on the wallpaper. They were arranged in parallel rows from floor to ceiling. One, two, three, four . . . . The paper was silvery white and when the sun shone on it, it had an hypnotic effect if you counted the flowers.

"I won't have the Inspector bothered with business as yet, Superintendent. He's far from well. Nerves . . . ."

The sight of Tordopp got on his nerves far more than Bowater's innocuous prattle. The doctor couldn't believe they hadn't got all the bits of cloth out of the wound at the cottage hospital and kept poking about with it trying to get foreign bodies out of it. He seemed, somehow, to resent Littlejohn's quick recovery and to want to prolong the agony.

"*I'm* not getting on his nerves, am I, Littlejohn?"

Bowater was quite plaintive.

"Of course not . . . ."

"I'm trying to help. Relieve him of anxiety."

Tordopp's nose flushed with temper. He looked like Donald Duck!

"I've said I won't have him upset and I mean it. Now, Superintendent, I'll be much obliged . . . I want to dress the wound . . . ."

Poor Bowater made an undignified exit. Mrs. Littlejohn saw him off the premises and mollified him on the way to the hotel door, whilst Tordopp peevishly examined the wound and seemed annoyed to find it healing well.

"You can try getting up for half an hour to-morrow, after I've been, Inspector. And see that you're not disturbed by callers pestering you about this murder case. Let the bishop rest for a bit. There's plenty of time for him when we've got you right. Now remember . . . ."

"I'll remember, doctor, thanks. Good morning."

"Good morning . . . ."

Tordopp looked surprised at the farewell. Was he being hustled out?

He was. For coming up the drive Littlejohn had spotted a taxi bringing Cromwell from his expeditions. It would never do for the doctor to know what was going on behind his back.

From where he was lying Littlejohn could see the foreshortened dark-clad form of his assistant climbing out of the vehicle. He watched him pay the driver in two instalments. First the fare; then the tip. The attitude of the taximan showed the latter mustn't have been much.

Before he could enter the hotel, however, Cromwell was hailed and pounced upon by another black figure. It was the priest, Father O'Shaughnessy, looking like a large cockroach from so far away.

Littlejohn could see the priest telling a long tale to Cromwell who looked ready to bolt at first and then froze to attention. Both parties gesticulated and pointed with their free hands. In the others they held their hats and the priest busily fanned himself with his own. He must have been running hard by the look of things.

Cromwell spoke vigorously to the clergyman, pointed to the hotel, called back the taxi and was driven off in the reverse direction.

There was a hasty tap on the bedroom door shortly afterwards and Mrs. Littlejohn opened it.

Father O'Shaughnessy, red-faced and panting, stood on the mat. He had recovered some of his smooth urbanity on the way up.

"I really ought to have called earlier to see you, Inspector. But I didn't know till this morning what had happened. I'm very sorry."

His blue eyes glowed with excitement behind his gold-framed glasses and his fat little hands twitched like fishes dying out of water. His neck was the same width as his head and bulged from his exertions like an inflated rubber tube.

"That's all right, father. But it seems you have other things to tell me, judging from what I've just seen from the window."

"You were watching us, were you? I was just reporting to your colleague that I've come from a walk across the golf-links and there found the body of Harry Keast. He's been murdered . . . ."

"Good God!"

Mrs. Littlejohn clicked her tongue against her teeth. Such language in front of a priest!

"Yes. I told Mr. Cromwell and he's gone to the police station for Superintendent Bowater. He asked me to telephone them as well, then they could arrange for the doctor and ambulance. Then I was to tell you what has happened and that Mr. Cromwell would be back as soon as possible."

"Where did you find the body, father?"

"Near Bolter's Hole. I was passing there with Mr. Shearwater when it happened. There weren't any players actually on the hole, but the last pair had been there about a quarter of an hour before. They saw poor Keast there brushing the fairway. He's been helping the green-keepers lately . . . ."

"You soon found that out."

"Well, you see, I passed those who'd last seen him, finishing their game as I ran for help, leaving Shearwater on guard behind. They were astonished . . . ."

"They hadn't seen anybody about?"

"No. I believe *you* were shot by a .44 rifle. So was Keast. Only the murderer took better aim than in your case. Poor Keast got it between the eyes. He was what you might call a sitting target. Probably leaning, as I've often seen him, resting on his besom."

"Did anyone hear the report?"

"Yes, I did. I saw Keast fall, too. I also judged where the shot had been fired from . . . . The other side of Bolter's Hole among the rocks at the edge . . . ."

What a man Father O'Shaughnessy was for springing a climax!

" . . . I ran round before I came away and found this . . . ."

The priest thereupon opened a spotless white handkerchief and threw from it into Littlejohn's lap a spent .44 cartridge.

"But there wasn't a soul in sight. Our man had evidently scrambled down the rocks and off hot-foot. I haven't handled the cartridge and I told Shearwater distinctly to see that nobody went near where I found it. And now I must be off and see what else I can do to help. I hope you'll soon be about again, Inspector . . . ."

And with that, the amazing little man bade them both good day, bowed himself out and toddled off.

They had installed a telephone in Littlejohn's room at his own request and a furious ringing heralded Cromwell on the other end.

"Did you get the priest's message, sir?"

"Yes. Where are you?"

"Telephoning from the golf clubhouse. They're just bringing along the body. Sorry I had to run away . . . ."

"That's all right. Anything interesting after all your enquiries?"

"Yes, sir. That's what I rang up about. I'll be right along and tell you, because it's hot. You know that chap Rupert Creer, the one who gave a village girl a baby almost on the eve of his wedding and became a sort of remittance man in South Africa . . . ?"

"Yes. What about him?"

"He's back in England, changed his name and living . . . guess where?"

"Come on. This isn't a quizz programme . . . ."

"Right in this town. I'll tell you how I traced it when I see you."

"What's he call himself?"

"Shearwater . . . ."

"My God! That's the chap the priest left minding the body!"

Littlejohn flung the travelling rug from his knees.

"Pass me that walking-stick, Letty . . . ."

Mrs. Littlejohn threw down her knitting in dismay.

"Whatever for . . . ? Remember what Dr. Tordopp . . . "

"Damn Tordopp! I'm getting up. I'm sorry to be rude, Letty, but really . . . ."

Mrs. Littlejohn passed him the stick with a smile.

He only reached the bedroom door and then had to give it up and sit down.

But his wife didn't say I told you so . . . .

Chapter Twelve
Country Ramble

CROMWELL began the day by a council of war with Prickwillow. They held it at the gate of the cottage hospital and their air of earnest preoccupation caused somewhat of a stir in a village where nothing much out of the ordinary ever seemed to happen.

Women peeped round the curtains at them and the more curious ones passed and repassed the absorbed couple on fantastic and fabulous errands in the hope of overhearing something as they went by.

"The bank'll just have opened, sir, if that's where you want to call first," said Prickwillow. "Topham, the clerk-in-charge, will probably help you willingly . . . ."

"Topham?" muttered Cromwell consulting his black notebook. "The vicar told Inspector Littlejohn it was Tiplady . . . ."

"Uh, uh, uh. A little way the vicar has of mixin' up names. Take it from me, it's Topham, sir."

"Right. I'll call there right away. Now, Prickwillow, I'd like you to go round to Cranage Farm and try to find out where they all were when somebody took a shot at the Inspector. Get to know if they have a .44 rifle, as well, if you can."

"Very good, sir, I'll do my best. As far as I know, there's no rifle. Shot guns, yes. Rifles, no."

"How do you know that?"

"Well . . . I get around. And during the war we 'ad details of all shot guns and rifles in this area. L.D.V. and Home Guard, you know."

"Yes. But they might have bought one since."

"Maybe. But they must have kept it very dark . . . ."

"Where would they get one, if they wanted one?"

"At Greyle, sir. That's the nearest big town with a gun-smith's shop. But why should they buy one? They didn't know all this was goin' to happen. They didn't know Inspector Littlejohn was coming. They didn't know they'd be takin' a pot-shot at 'im, even granted they did it. I don't think . . . "

That seemed reasonable enough and well argued.

"Anyhow, see what you can find out, constable."

They strolled towards the bank. A sub-branch of the London and South Counties established in what looked like a small disused Village Hall.

"This foundation stone was laid by

Sir Hector H. L. Creer, D.L., J.P.

Sept. 26th, 1888."

"That reminds me," said Cromwell. "Do the Creers still live in these parts?"

"No, sir. Family impoverished by death duties and the main line died out. Mrs. Macintosh had another sister who died and, of course, Mr. Rupert went away. They sold the place to a man called Pybus, a new-rich. Pybus's Potato Crackles . . . . You'll have heard of them . . . ."

"Never had the pleasure. So it's no use looking into that side of the case."

"No, sir. Mr. Pybus 'ud be delighted to show you round the 'all. Collects pictures and antiques. Quite a museum. But what good would that do? Wastin' time, wouldn't it?"

"You've said it. Well, let's be getting on then. You to Cranage, Prickwillow. Me to the bank. I'll 'phone you when I get back, because if there's time, I might go to Greyle."

"'Bus leaves every two hours. Takes just over half an hour there. If you was to catch the twelve o'clock, you could get a bit o' something to eat in Greyle. You'll not find much here . . . . Then perhaps come back on the four o'clock."

"Right. I'll see about it, then. Now . . . let's get crackin'."

They parted and some of the idlers of the village looked ready to follow them, but decided against it and, sitting on a seat in the centre under a large tree, began to spin their own theories about the shooting and who had done it.

The bank was a small, low-ceilinged room, simply furnished. A counter, a screen separating the clerks' desk from the banking part, a cubby-hole for private consultations. The clerk-in-charge was sitting behind the screen drinking a cup of tea and his companion, a guard, was dusting the place. There wasn't enough work even for one man and the guard was there to see that nobody ran away with the clerk or the cash.

The public side of the screen was covered with posters, like a hoarding. Buy Savings Certificates. Open a Savings Account; Deposits from £1 upwards. Bankers' Notice to the Public. Collection of Cheques. Are You Keeping the Roads Safe? Foreign Business Transacted. Boatmen's National Bank of New York; Travellers' Cheques Accepted; *Sont acceptés ici.*

Cromwell liked the little bit of French.

"Yes, sir?"

Mr. Topham looked cautiously at Cromwell and his foot drew a little nearer the stud under the counter which operated the alarm-bell hanging on the wall outside. Not that the bell did much good. Last time he trod on the button by mistake the yokels had looked up and said, "Tryin' out the 'larum," and gone on with their smoking.

All the same, you never know.

"Yes, sir."

"Mr. Topham? The vicar sent me to see you."

Cromwell thought that would put Topham at his ease, but it didn't. The vicar was always sending somebody strange. On the strength of 'Foreign Business Transacted' he'd once sent a Latvian refugee who couldn't speak English and they'd had an awful job getting rid of him. And then last week, he'd introduced an insurance tout, who stayed trying to convince Topham that he might drop dead any minute and leave a suffering wife and family, when all the time Topham wasn't married. Talked about wise and foolish virgins and having one's can full of oil in emergencies . . . .

Mr. Topham looked apprehensive. He looked more so when Cromwell handed over his card.

"I believe, Mr. Topham, your bank has something to do with making remittances to a Mr. Rupert Creer in South Africa. Could you tell me if he's still out there?"

"I'll have to consult central office," he said. "Wilkins, get me Greyle, will you, please?"

In all matters except paying and receiving cash in the ordinary course of business, Mr. Topham had to consult. He consulted the authorities at Greyle on banking, his domineering mother on affairs of heart, three stockbrokers about his surplus income, and, in secret, Old Moore's Almanac about the future.

"They're on," said Wilkins laconically.

Mr. Topham shut himself in a telephone box and Cromwell could see him anxiously putting his case to higher authority. A tall, lean man of about forty, grey haired, face lined with worry, long nervous hands, thin, scraggy neck and big nose. He hadn't got on in the bank because before he'd even reached the entrance age, his mother had sapped him of all initiative and will of his own. In the bank he was a cipher. But life has compensations. On the links he was a giant. Handicap : Plus One. Topham didn't know how he did it. He must have been born so. He won the bank golf cup every year and all the directors and all the directors' men couldn't stop him.

Mr. Topham emerged from his glass case.

"Yes," he said, returning to the counter. "Our trustee department still make payments for the account of Mr. Creer. They pay them over to the branch of the South African bank in London . . . ."

"Thank you. Anything more?"

"I thought that was all you wanted to know . . . ."

"I'm anxious to find out as much about Mr. Creer as I can. Will I have to go over to Greyle to get fuller details . . . ?"

"I'm afraid you will. Although the accounts of the Creer family are connected with this little office, all the business is done by the trustee department in Greyle. The family died out or such as was left of it removed from the locality . . . ."

"I see. Any use my telephoning your people in Greyle? I'll show you my warrant-card here to put things right and you can tell your people it's O.K. to give me information. Right?"

"I'll consult . . . Get Greyle again, will you, Wilkins, please?"

The guard, who looked like an ex-pug., rose obediently like one in a dream and heavily entered the telephone cabin.

"They're on . . . "

Topham told his tale again, listened carefully to what someone said and then passed the receiver to Cromwell.

"Trustee Department, Greyle. Are you a police officer?"

"Yes. I'm wondering if you'd be so good as to give me a bit of information about Mr. Rupert Creer . . . ."

The voice assumed an officious quack.

"We're not allowed to disclose anything confidential, you know. You'll have to bring a court order . . . ."

"I guess this won't be confidential. All I want to know is, do you still make remittances to South Africa for Mr. Rupert Creer?"

"Yes, we do. Why?"

"I'm trying to trace him. He's the late Bishop of Greyle's brother-in-law, you know . . . ."

"I'm aware of that."

The voice wasn't going to allow outsiders to teach it anything about the hierarchy of Greyle. No, sir.

"Can you help me then, sir?"

"I have already told you, we still make the payments . . . "

The voice was rich and arrogant, with a mellow fruity note, like a trombone played with a hat on the end of it. Cromwell imagined its owner to be small, plump, well-fed, and a bit pickled in port or brandy . . . . Actually, the man was tall, thin and a rabid teetotaller, but that has nothing to do with the case . . . .

" . . . . You make the payments to a London bank, sir. Have you Mr. Creer's address . . . ?"

"I don't think . . . "

"Look here, sir. Are you or aren't you going to cooperate? Are you the manager?"

"No . . . I'm chief clerk . . . ."

"Put me on to the manager, please . . . ."

"I . . . I . . . Very well . . . ."

Another pause and then a different voice. This time calm and clerical, with a faint touch of sedate jocularity.

"Queasey here . . . . What can I do for you?"

"You the manager, sir?"

"Yes . . . ."

Mr. Queasey was a model of tact and sound judgment. As head of what was known internally as "Stiffs Department,"Mr. Queasey had, in the course of his duties, to circulate among the bereaved of Greyle. And to circulate among the bereaved of Greyle was itself a feat. Clerical bigwigs, ecclesiastical trusts, sacerdotal hangers-on and snobs all pressed upon him with queer claims and importunities which would not be denied.

"Oh yes. We still make the remittance for Mr. Rupert Creer. Funds left in trust for him by his family . . . . No. Don't know the fellah's address now. London Bank deal with that. Eh? Oh yes. Pioneers Bank of South Africa, Threadneedle Street . . . . Want to know something from them? Yes . . . . Oh, that's quite all right. Always ready to further interests of justice. As a matter of fact, I'll telephone 'em if you like. Won't take above five minutes. Right. Ring you back . . . ."

Cromwell returned to the counter and Mr. Topham tried to entertain him in conversation whilst Mr. Queasey telephoned to the South African bank in London.

"Play golf, sergeant?"

"No, can't say I do. Busy . . . too busy for games. Play a bit of clock-golf when I take my holidays . . . ."

Mr. Topham shut-up about golf. He tried detective stories.

"You chaps must have some exciting adventures. I read a lot of thrillers. Not much to do here. It passes the time . . . ."

"I guess it does . . . ."

"Yes. But facts are stranger than fiction, aren't they? I'll bet you Scotland Yard fellows could tell some tales if they'd only let you . . . ."

"Oh," said Cromwell modestly . . . . When he tries to look modest his face is a picture . . . . "Oh, I don't know. A bit humdrum and routine, you know. You get used to it."

"What do you think about a lot of these thrillers, sergeant?"

"Weeeell . . . Thing that strikes me is there's more money in imagining crimes than in actually solving 'em on the spot. And what makes me laugh is the number of detectives there are. All big shots at Scotland Yard. Hundreds of 'em. Why, we'd need Buckingham Palace, the Houses of Parliament and half the buildings in London to house them . . . ."

"Still, that's beside the point, really, isn't it? What I mean is, your cases for example, would . . . "

The telephone rang. Cromwell was relieved.

Mr. Topham ran into the box, then ran out again.

"Greyle . . . " he said cryptically, for a villager had just come in for change for half-a-crown.

Mr. Queasey had the information for Cromwell.

The London bank had been very communicative. At first they'd sent Mr. Creer's money out to South Africa . . . to one of their Rhodesian branches. But after the war he'd come back to England. His account was with them in London now. They'd supplied his address, too. He was trading as James Shearwater, Agent, Main Street, Port Mervin.

Cromwell thanked Mr. Queasey very much and Mr. Queasey said it was a pleasure and come again if he could assist. They bowed one another off the 'phone . . . .

"Good-bye, Mr. Topham and thanks very much for your very timely help . . . ."

"Oh, it's a pleasure. Very interesting indeed to be mixed up in a Scotland Yard investigation. I shall look out for results in the papers. Are you in charge of it?"

"Oh, no. Littlejohn's on the case. My chief. You'll have heard of him, won't you?"

"I can't say I have . . . ."

"Good Lord! Where were you brought up?" said Cromwell and the swing door closed between them, leaving Topham to think it out in his spare time.

Chapter Thirteen
Cathedral Close

IT was a horrible journey from Medhope to Greyle. The secondary road was full of potholes and the 'Bus was driven by a madman. Passengers got on and off all the way and the driver couldn't wait for the bell. He was away like a shot leaving everybody to scramble to their seats as best they could. Swinging like a crowd of startled monkeys on the upright stays or cakewalking along the gangway like crazy jive dancers. Cromwell mentioned the matter to the conductor.

"Best driver in the service," came the contemptuous reply. "Knows his onions, does Ken."

"God help us when the worst driver takes over then," said Cromwell, bouncing up and down on his seat like a Jack-in-the-box.

Cromwell reported Ken at the 'Bus station. Not that that would do any good, except to precipitate an unofficial strike, but it gave the sergeant a bit of satisfaction to voice his grievances.

Then he made his way to Dr. Mulroy's surgery.

The road lay along the High Street, which sloped steeply from the level of the water-meadows which lay around Greyle, up to the cathedral, standing on its rock and seeming to sail away among the great billowing clouds like a stately ship at sea.

The steep street ended in a flat plateau on which rose the beautiful twin-towered church surrounded by an inner ring of buildings, which formed the close.

The afternoon was sunny and so hot that you could hardly bear to walk outside the shade of buildings. The heat had softened the macadam of the roadway and higher up where it changed to cobble-stones had raised the tar between the setts in shining black bubbles. Nevertheless the city was animated as though everyone had become full of vitality from the pleasantness of the weather and the brightness of the sun. Instead of taking siestas from the heat, people were striding along the pavements and surging in and out of shops in crowds.

Two or three charabancs full of trippers honked their way up the High Street and discharged their cargoes outside the close. You could see the excursionists hunting for pubs and restaurants before settling down to the rounds of the cathedral and other relics.

There was an outer ring of large houses back-to-back with the ecclesiastical buildings in the close and among these Cromwell found Mulroy's consulting rooms. The place had at one time been a stately dwelling-house, now divided into suites, mainly let to doctors, dentists and other healers of one kind and another.

A broad, graceful staircase rose from a wide square hall to the upper rooms. The door of one of the latter bore a small plate, "Dr. Mulroy."

It was outside consulting hours and the receptionist looked surprised to see a visitor. She seemed new to the job and studied Cromwell's card a minute or two before making up her mind what to do. Then she disappeared into an inner room.

The place had an air of overdone opulence about it, like the suite of a second-rate company promoter without much taste. A Chinese carpet which must have cost hundreds, somehow didn't just tone with the Queen Anne dining-suite and heavy sideboard. Neither did the parchment shades of the two standard lamps. And why the dining-room furniture at all in a doctor's waiting-room? It didn't seem to make sense.

The receptionist returned. She had a peculiar walk. One foot behind the other like a tightrope artiste quickly crossing the wire. In the street below you could hear the trippers wandering about, shouting at each other.

"We've to meet the charabanc here at half-past five . . . ."

"Dr. Mulroy will see you," said the girl, tightroped back to the inner door with Cromwell and opened it for him. Dr. Mulroy rose from a large desk to meet him, hand extended.

Cromwell had never been in the company of a psychiatrist before. His only experience of that kind of thing had been at music halls and variety shows, where hypnotists had got to work on members of the audience, put them to sleep and then made them do all sorts of tricks. Bray like donkeys, scratch and caper like monkeys, stand on their heads and think they were Napoleon or the Prime Minister. He expected a tall, lean man with piercing eyes and a will of iron and braced himself for a mental tussle. He received a shock.

Dr. Mulroy was small, fat, well-washed, and full of unction with a trace of furtiveness about it. Not that he was without confidence. He radiated self-assurance and prosperity. Cromwell took an instinctive dislike to him from the start and set his mind firmly against being bamboozled or mesmerised, as he called it in his own thoughts.

The second room was like the first. Overdone. There was none of the utilitarian efficiency usually found in specialists' consulting rooms. The desk was too large and impressive. The chairs too plump and self-satisfied looking. The armchairs too deep and comfortable. Dr. Mulroy looked too deep and comfortable too.

The psychiatrist extended a podgy well-kept hand. Cromwell took and shook it. It was like gripping a pneumatic glove. You couldn't feel any bones in it.

Through the open window you could still hear the trippers bawling at one another outside. They had been drinking and their voices were fruity and confused.

"We've found a good shop for tea . . . . Come on into th' cathedral and we'll . . . "

"Good afternoon, sergeant. Nothing unpleasant, I hope . . . ."

Mulroy washed his hands in air. Optimism oozing from every pore. All the same, he looked a bit uncomfortable, as though wondering what he'd done wrong.

"I'd just like to ask you a question or two about the late Bishop of Greyle, doctor. I believe he was a collaborator of yours in some research . . . ."

Collaborator. Good word, thought Cromwell. It seemed to come on his tongue from nowhere and pleased him immensely.

Mulroy looked pleased and relieved, too.

"Ah . . . . Sit down, sergeant. May I offer you a cigarette . . . ?"

The doctor sat down and crossed his prosperous hands one over the other.

"Now . . . "

"I believe, sir, that the late bishop . . . "

Here the corners of Dr. Mulroy's mouth turned down and he made a little flapping gesture with his hands. The equivalent of doffing one's hat when a corpse passes . . . .

" . . . that the late bishop was working with you on some problem or other in mental work. I'm no expert, sir, but could you tell me exactly what you were at?"

Mulroy pursed his lips, raised his eyebrows and bounced the tips of his little fat fingers together.

"Well . . . It's rather difficult to the layman. You see, it's a case of opening up the unconscious depths of the mind. We have achieved this by a technique we call psycho-analysis . . . ."

His voice grew patronising, like an adult teaching a child new truths. Cromwell couldn't make out the half of what he was talking about, but somehow out of all the jargon managed to boil down a core of common sense. He had to raise his voice to get a word in edgeways, for Mulroy, once started, was like a river in spate.

"Excuse me, doctor. You're just telling me that the bishop and you were trying out old methods from the East to reach the same results as new methods in the West?"

Mulroy looked surprised and a bit annoyed. It is exasperating to spend years studying a subject and mastering its terms and then suddenly find the apparently ignorant layman intuitively knows as much as you do.

"Yes," he said, sharply. He couldn't say anything else.

"And he was starving to produce the condition in himself that the Indian fakirs, say, produce by fasting and such?"

"Yes. But . . . "

Cromwell raised his hand, like a traffic policeman holding up a stream of cars.

"Excuse me, sir. Would that treatment of himself affect his mind at all?"

"Well. Yes and no."

"What do you mean, sir?"

Cromwell felt he had somehow taken the upper hand in the interview. This mental chap, as he called himself, wasn't as confident as he tried to make out. In fact, there seemed something just a bit phoney about him.

"One cannot undertake exacting work of that kind without strain. The bishop taxed himself so much that he had to take a rest. That was the reason for his going to the seaside. To recuperate . . . "

"On your advice?"

"Yes, and on that of his own doctor . . . ."

"You're not his doctor, then?"

"No, no. I'm a specialist, not a general practitioner. As soon as the bishop showed signs of strain, I advised him to see Dr. Packard, his own man."

"I see. In the course of your association, did the bishop ever mention being in any danger at all . . . ?"

Mulroy raised his hands in protest.

"Never, I assure you."

"Have you known the bishop long, sir?"

"About four years. Although we didn't start our collaboration until last year."

"What brought you together in the matter?"

Mulroy looked a bit indignant. He was used to asking the questions, not others, and he didn't feel comfortable when the boot was on the other foot. The blood mounted to his forehead, but he mastered his feelings.

"I have many patients among the cathedral set and they mentioned my work to the bishop. Really, sergeant, I don't see where all this is getting us . . . ."

Cromwell rose and took up his bowler hat.

"Neither do I, sir. But I hoped in the course of our conversation something might come out which would help us in our investigation of the murder . . . ."

"I'm sure the ordinary day to day work we did, searching for the truth and healing light, had nothing whatever to do with the bishop's unhappy end in a distant place. And now, sergeant, my consulting time is approaching and I'm afraid . . . "

"Sorry to have taken so much of your time, sir."

"Don't mention it, sergeant. Eager to help, I'm sure. But you realise that there's nothing here . . . "

Cromwell's hand was on the door knob.

"No, sir. Many thanks all the same."

He descended the staircase slowly. 'Healing light,' the doctor had said. It didn't sound professional somehow. More like New Thought and spiritual healing than medical psychology. He shrugged his shoulders. Probably so much messing and probing with queer patients had made Mulroy a bit queer, too.

Just as Cromwell reached the ground-floor hall, a small door under the stairs opened and a man in a boiler-suit emerged. He looked to have been up the flue.

"Dirty job?" asked Cromwell with his wintery smile.

"Aye. Just been cleanin' out the flues of the heatin' stove. Plumbers is comin' in next week to put some new plates in. Allus something wrong with that boiler. Pay 'em to get a new 'un. But they won't be told . . . ."

"You caretaker here?"

"Aye. Live in a bit of a flat on top. You cap hardly turn round in it."

"Bit different from some of the suites. Dr. Mulroy's, say."

"Aye. Then I don't coin money like he does. His place is always full of patients. Women mostly. Women with nothin' much to do but think theirselves ill. An' they come 'ere to talk to Dr. Mulroy about themselves and their troubles and pay 'im handsome for doin' it. Wish I could come by money as easy. Nothin' but bed and work here, and very few thankyous."

You couldn't make out the varying expressions of the man's face properly, as the grime blotted them out. All you could see were the watery pale eyes with exaggerated whites, the eyebrows and rather straggly moustache filmed with soot and ashes, and the loose red mouth relaxing and tightening, probably at the thoughts of a drink. He was wearing dirty carpet slippers.

"Did the late bishop come here quite a lot?"

"Oh aye. Here about twice a week to see Mulroy. What for, I don't know. Shouldn't think they'd much in common. Anyhow, they'd a few words the night before the bishop went off and got 'imself killed."

"A quarrel, you say?"

Cromwell pricked up his ears. This was going to be good.

"Well . . . Not exactly a quarrel. Not like *that* anyhow . . . ."

With a dirty paw the janitor indicated a couple slanging each other for all they were worth in the street. A pair of visitors, and the man had either been taking too much drink or making eyes at another woman.

"Disgustin' I call it. For two pins, I'd go 'ome. Away two hours an' look at you!"

Their voices rose and fell.

"Not like them two. More controlled, if you see what I mean. But as he stood to go at the open door, the bishop didn't half tell off old Mulroy. 'Money under false pretences, Mulroy,' he sez. 'And I intend to see it doesn't 'appen agen. Mrs. Polglaze is a poor woman. She can't afford to be paying like that without results . . . "'

"Whose Mrs. Polglaze?"

"Widder of one of the minor canons. Lives in rooms not far from here. Has a daughter who's not quite right in her head."

"I see. And did the daughter come here to Dr. Mulroy?"

"Regular. Guess it was what he charged the old girl for it that caused the row."

"Where does the old lady live, did you say?"

The man took Cromwell to the front door and showed him. Passers-by looked astonished at the strange, sooty apparition embellishing the front of such an opulent block.

"First to the right; first to left; then ask. Everybody knows the old lady . . . . Thank you. I'll get a drink with it as soon as I've washed off some o' this stuff. Thirsty work up them flues . . . ."

Mrs. Polglaze had two rooms in a tall, narrow house converted into tenements. Impoverished gentility. Cromwell felt very sorry for her. He saw nothing of the ailing daughter, and didn't ask where she was. The old lady was tall, angular and frail. She looked resigned to poverty and even the charity of those among whom she had once moved as an equal.

"Yes. My daughter has not been well for some time. I've done my best for her . . . ."

"I just called to ask how she was. The late bishop, you know, was very interested in her case and I feel . . . "

He didn't know how to go on. He'd impulsively gone to see the old lady following the caretaker's information and hoped to improvise to suit the occasion. Now he couldn't think what to say. He felt like taking to his heels and beating a retreat. But his bowler and gloomy suit of black saved him. He was mistaken for the secretary of a discreet charity.

"I believe she's been under Dr. Mulroy . . . ."

"Yes. He was recommended by the dean's wife, but I'm afraid didn't do my daughter much good. I had to give it up. It cost too much. The fees were very high. Sixty guineas for a quarter's treatment. Of course, I grant the visits took a long time. Sometimes over an hour of the doctor's time. But I couldn't afford. I had to sell some of my remaining funds . . . ."

"Dear me. I'm sorry about that. Did the bishop get to know of it?"

"Yes. He seemed annoyed. He said he'd speak to the doctor about it. I urged him not to. I didn't wish . . . "

"Quite . . . ."

That was all there was to it. Cromwell would have liked to leave a pound or two behind for the old lady. But she wasn't the sort you did that to. So he shook her hand, bade her good-bye and remembered her and her plight for weeks after the visit.

It was late afternoon when Cromwell left the building. He hadn't had any food and he found there was no connection that night to get him back to Mervin. So he telephoned to Mrs. Littlejohn at her hotel, learned they'd got Littlejohn safely installed, and told her he would be in on the morrow. Then he took a room at a small pub near the close.

There was a public library nearby and he turned in to find out what he could about Mulroy. He asked for the Medical Directory.

The assistant handed him a little-used volume. Cromwell couldn't find Mulroy in it at all. The assistant seeing his baffled face asked if he'd found what he wanted and then volunteered to help if she could.

It ended by the Head Librarian being consulted. He soon settled the matter.

"Oh, Mulroy. He's not a medical man at all. An American Ph.D., Doctor of Philosophy. Got all the airs and graces of a fully-fiedged medico and makes twice as much as most of 'em. Speaking between ourselves, he's a bit of a quack . . . a catchpenny . . . ."

Cromwell slowly strolled away. The visit to Greyle hadn't been very fruitful. A little fake of a doctor and his quarrel with the bishop for robbing widows. All the same, according to the janitor, the bishop had mentioned 'false pretences' . . .

A bell was vigorously clanging from the cathedral as Cromwell made his way to his hotel. A loafer told him it was the curfew.

"Good Lord! And I haven't eaten yet," said Cromwell.

The loafer gazed after him and then turning to his pal, tapped his forehead with a grimy index.

Chapter Fourteen
The Man Who Came Back

HARRY KEAST'S body had been removed to the town morgue and Bowater's men had minutely examined the scene of the crime and found nothing to reward their efforts.

The Superintendent was in Littlejohn's room reciting all the details in a bewildered, apologetic fashion. He seemed to feel that he was responsible for the lack of clues. Before his arrival Cromwell had given his chief a brief report on his labours since they parted.

"It's quite obvious that we must concentrate our enquiries here in Mervin," said Littlejohn. "With Harry Keast shot dead on our doorstep it's no use running far and wide and wasting our energies."

They were having afternoon tea at a table by the window. It was warm and sunny outside. The fuss created by Keast's violent death had died down. Father O'Shaughnessy and Shearwater had just come in and had joined the rest in the lounge for tea. People had settled down to their holiday routine again. Nothing exciting might have happened. The hotel lounge had a large alcoved bow-window and from where he was sitting, Littlejohn could see the priest and his companion drinking their tea and telling a long tale to the assembled guests.

"One thing I'd like you to do, Bowater. Get some of your men on thoroughly examining Bolter's Hole at low tide. And you go with them, Cromwell, please. Nothing might result from it. On the other hand, you might strike something . . . ."

"Such as . . . ?" said Bowater. He was out of his depth entirely.

"I don't quite know. But it's been the centre of two murders now and we've neglected the topography of that part a bit. Meanwhile, could I see Shearwater? Don't let the priest come with him. I want a word with him alone."

Mrs. Littlejohn had gone for tea downstairs by way of a change and the two police officers left Littlejohn alone as they went off to their jobs. The Inspector gazed vacantly through the window and down the road which ran along the quayside and finally petered out in a path leading to the golf-links. They were improving and widening the road and there was a watchman there at night to keep an eye on the roadmenders' tackle. He had just come on duty and was busy overhauling and filling the red lamps. Littlejohn's eyes narrowed and he nodded to himself . . . .

There was a knock on the door.

"Come in," called the Inspector, and gulped down the last of his tea. A moment's hesitation and then the door opened. It was Shearwater.

He looked greyer and more bent than ever.

"Good evening, sir."

"Good evening, Inspector."

Shearwater was apprehensive. You could tell by the tone of his voice that he expected the worst.

"Sit down, Mr. Shearwater. Just a word or two about this fresh murder. You were with Father O'Shaughnessy when it happend, I believe."

"Yes, we were together. I stayed with the body when O'Shaughnessy went for help."

"Have you known the priest long?"

"No. We met about a fortnight ago. Both on our own, so got friendly."

Littlejohn filled his pipe slowly.

"Do you mind passing me the matches from the table there? Thanks. How long have you been in Mervin, Mr. Shearwater?"

"A little over six months. Why?"

Shearwater had been a bit apathetic until now, but suddenly realised that he was being questioned instead of allowed to tell his tale of the afternoon's happenings. He looked put-out.

"Why am I being questioned on personal matters? It's nothing to do with the case, has it? I'm not suspected . . . ."

"No. But the bishop was your brother-in-law, wasn't he?"

You could have heard a pin drop. Outside the guests were scattering after tea. Father O'Shaughnessy appeared among the loungers on the terrace. He cast his eye up to Littlejohn's room and waved at the inspector. The priest certainly didn't miss much.

"Who told you that?"

Shearwater was trying to bluff it out, but his very manner answered the question.

"Never mind. You are Mr. Rupert Creer, aren't you, sir?"

"I was. But I changed my name legally. The family didn't want anything to do with me; and I was the same about them. I changed it to make a clean start."

"When did you return from . . . let me see, Africa, was it?"

"Yes. Rhodesia. About six months ago, I said."

"And came right here."

"Had a week or two in London making arrangements and then settled in Mervin. Where is all this leading to?"

"Did you meet your sister and brother-in-law when they were here?"

"I met my sister, but not the bishop."

"That's funny, isn't it?"

"I kept out of his way. He always disliked me. It wasn't difficult dodging James. His routine was very fixed. He went out a lot walking alone."

"Where?"

"Mainly the golf-links and beyond. It's very quiet and he seemed to want it quiet."

"You met your sister, you say. Often?"

"Two or three times. I tried to keep out of her way, too, but we bumped into each other one day on the stairs. I've changed a bit but she recognised me at once."

"You told her you'd be keeping out of the bishop's way?"

"Naturally . . . ."

The evening sun was hot and the view across the water very beautiful. Littlejohn sighed and wished he could have had a peaceful holiday. All this mix-up . . . ! He leaned and opened the casement, letting in the noises of the quay. The watchman was still clattering about with his lamps and one of the yachts moored to the jetty had a wireless-set going. Dance music. People were trying to dance a bit on the deck on which you couldn't whip a cat round.

"Did your sister tell you anything about your brother-in-law?"

"Oh, they were here for a rest for him. He'd been overdoing it. I did see him without speaking to him. He looked a bit queer to me."

"What do you mean, sir?"

"A bundle of nerves . . . "

"Naturally. He was here for nervous strain."

"Yes, but it looked more than that. They've always been a queer family, the Macintoshes. Jim had a sort of tick of the face. Kept twitching and I saw him sort of kicking himself on the calf with the other foot as he walked. You know, just as though he were itching and rubbing it. You know what I mean . . . ."

"Yes. And those long walks alone. Did you ever meet him?"

"No. Why should I? Look here, are you thinking I killed him? Because I've got an alibi. Father O'Shaughnessy . . . "

"Yes, I know. He's your alibi for both murders. He was putting you to bed when the first occurred and walking with you when Keast was killed."

"Yes. Why should I want to murder my brother-in-law? I grant we didn't hit it but . . . "

"What about the bishop, though? You gave him little reason for liking you. In fact, I should think he'd hate the very sight of you."

"What's somebody been telling you?"

"I know why you left the country years ago, Mr. Shearwater."

"Well, I'd nothing to do with either of the crimes, so, if you don't mind, I'll be going."

Life must have dealt hardly with Creer, alias Shearwater. The man whom Littlejohn had imagined as a gay philanderer in his young days had become prematurely aged and timid and shifty-looking. A bit of a soak, too, from all accounts.

As he reached the door, however, Shearwater drew himself up. His dull eyes glinted as he faced Littlejohn and he squared his shoulders.

"I did hear," he said clearly. "I did hear that Jim got a bit rough on Evelyn in his queer moods. Didn't speak to her for days and neglected her. By God! if he'd touched a hair of her head I would have killed him. She's had quite enough with that family . . . ."

"What do you mean, quite enough?"

"Have you seen her?"

"Yes . . . ."

"And have you seen his family?"

"Yes, why?"

"Once there wasn't a more vivacious girl in the county. Riding, dancing, high-spirits . . . . All the Creers were that way. What was she when you saw her? A faded, tired, middle-aged woman. The Macintoshes did that to her. Repressed and tortured her between them. What a different life she'd have had if she'd married Frank Tennant . . . ."

"Tennant? That Judge Tennant?"

"Yes. He wanted her, too. Still a bachelor."

"Has he been telling you things?"

"Certainly not. Frank's not that sort. But he'd have given her the place and happiness she ought to have had. He'd taste, position, culture, breadth of mind and above all, kindliness, sweet sanity and an outlook akin to Evelyn's. Now, if he still loves her, and I know he does, he can come into his own if it's not too late . . . ."

"You knew he was staying here?"

"Yes. He comes here a lot. Of course, I didn't know when I booked rooms here, any more than I knew that Evelyn and Jim were coming . . . ."

"Seems a bit of a coincidence . . . ."

"What are you getting at? I guess Tennant perhaps came to get a look at Evelyn and see was she all right, but I was established here when they all arrived."

Littlejohn sat alone for a bit when Shearwater had gone. The evening sun shone across the water like molten gold. A string of little pleasure boats bobbed across the bay and turned in to the harbour to tie-up for the night. They were still dancing on the yacht by the pier and the watchman on the road was trying to light a fire in his brazier.

A maid entered the room to clear away the tea-things.

"Just hand me that pad and pencil on the mantelpiece, will you, please?"

"Yes, sir."

"Littlejohn scribbled a note."

Mr. Littlejohn at the hotel would like a word or two with you. Come up right away. It will mean ten shillings for you.

"Please give that to a page, will you? Tell him to take it to the watchman down on the road there and bring him back with him and show him the way to my room."

"Very good, sir."

The maid looked surprised. What was the Inspector doing wanting a disreputable night-watchman up at Cape Mervin Hotel? She shrugged to herself, gathered the tea-things and left.

Littlejohn watched the page in his violet uniform hurry down the drive to the road. The watchman took the note hesitantly, turned it over and round and round in his hand and then decided to read it. It took a long time before he grasped what it was about. He seemed to be arguing the point with the page, who pointed back at the hotel. The man indicated his lamps and swept his arm in the direction of the barrows and shovels he was supposed to be guarding. Littlejohn smiled as he thought he wouldn't be quite so fussy and diligent when the pubs opened.

The man and boy were on their way, one brisk and trying to look haughty and businesslike; the other shambling along, slowly and a bit resentfully, as though showing he was making the journey under protest and just to oblige. The ten shillings had probably done the trick.

The watchman looked bewildered when he entered Littlejohn's room. So did Mrs. Littlejohn who had just come up to see that everything was all right.

"Sit down," said Littlejohn. "I'm a police Inspector and I'm seeking information about what happened on the road the night the Bishop of Greyle was murdered. Remember it?"

"I don't know anything about it," said the visitor.

He was a little man with an overgrowth of thick grey stubble covering the lower part and sides of his face. His eyes were pale blue and bleary and one looked to have a cataract growing over it. He wore corduroy trousers, an old serge jacket and twiddled his cap in his hands.

"You were on duty on the night of the crime?"

"Yes, but . . . "

"In your hut?"

"Yes, but . . . "

"Did you leave it at all?"

"Not after hal' past ten. I went fer a drink then, but come back and stopped . . . "

"Did anybody pass after that on the way to the golf links?"

"Yes, but . . . "

"But what?"

"They's allus a lot passes. Proper courtin' shop those links is. Me and me missus went up so long since. Goings-on up there . . . ."

"Never mind that. Did you know the Bishop of Greyle?"

"Not as such, but 'ad 'im pinted out to me. Didn't sort o' wear bishop's leggin's, but 'ad a purple dickey on instead of a black'un like other parsons . . . ."

"Did you see him pass your hut on the night of the crime?"

"No. It was dark. Too dark to reckernise anybody who passed."

There was something funny about the fellow. The way he set his mouth. His lips grew tight as each question was asked and he chewed the insides of his lips nervously before he answered. He looked like one who's been told to keep his mouth shut.

"Do you know Mr. Shearwater who's staying here?"

There was a flicker of hesitancy and then the man worked his jaws again, chewing away.

"No. Don't know nobody 'ere. Not my sort. Toffs, they're supposed to be, though to see what some of 'em do, you wouldn't think so."

"What do you mean?"

"Nothin'."

"Come on, now . . . ."

"Nothin'."

"Did you know Harry Keast?"

"Yes. Bloody shame somebody done 'im in . . . ."

"Who'd want to do him in?"

"Don't ask me. That's yore job to find out."

Still evasion. Like getting blood out of a stone.

"There's a telephone-box just at the hotel gates. Can you see it from your cabin?"

"Yes. Only patch o' light on the quay on this side after they put out the lights at eleven."

"Did you see anybody telephoning there on the night of the murder? Later on, I mean. Say about eleven."

The man didn't answer. He fumbled with his cap and looked down at his large boots.

"Come now. I promised you ten shillings, but this isn't earning it. You can't even answer a civil question properly."

The thought of losing his ten bob stung the man into a bit of activity. He thought gravely for a bit, his jaws still moving.

"Yes. I see somebody."

At last!

"Who was it?"

Littlejohn asked the question quietly, as though afraid to frighten the fellow back in his shell.

"'arry Keast."

"'Harry Keast!"

"Yes. Knew him by his cap. Plain as a . . . plain as a . . . Wore it back to front."

"H'm. Well here's your money and thank you for coming."

The man shambled off, wiping his lips with the back of his hand, stimulated no doubt by the spare cash. He didn't even say good night.

Littlejohn sunk his head on his chest. He was weary.

Lots of possibles, but no probables until suddenly, like a bolt from the blue, comes the tale of the man who telephoned. Harry Keast again. And Harry had got himself murdered that very afternoon!

Littlejohn asked Letty to telephone to Bowater and ask him to have the watchman watched, in case he tried to contact someone he was shielding.

"I expect he'll put a big, flatfooted bobby on the job, and scare the quarry off. So, please tell him to have his most inconspicuous plain-clothes chap on, will you? Watching the watchman! That's a good one. Like taking care of the caretaker's daughter while the caretaker's busy taking care . . . ."

"Whatever's the matter with you, Tom?"

"I don't quite know myself . . . ."

He certainly didn't. He felt light-headed a bit. But suddenly cheerful. Just as he always did before some bright thought or intuition on a case came to him.

"Run along and tell Bowater, there's a good girl."

He nodded off whilst she was away and she let him sleep a bit when she returned. The dinner gong wakened him. He looked through the window.

"My God! Come here, Letty . . . ."

Along the road from the town to the quay was approaching a plain-clothes man with 'copper' written over every inch of him. From where the Littlejohn's were watching, you could almost see his regulation boots.

With ostentatious nonchalance the officer approached the watchman's hut.

"Now what's he going to do?" said Littlejohn with a chuckle. He might not have been on the case, but watching a farce on the stage.

Still devil-may-care, the plain-clothes man entered the telephone kiosk and pretended to telephone, his eye all the time on the watchman. The latter was cooking a kipper on a spike over his fire and didn't notice anything.

Littlejohn hobbled down to dinner. The 'tec was still telephoning and the watchman, having cooked his kipper started to eat it with his fingers, gnawing bread from a large chunk to help it down.

Chapter Fifteen
The "Patrick Creegan"

HARRY KEAST'S home was one of a row of cottages in North Street. An untidy dark woman with a baby in her arms opened the door after Littlejohn knocked. She had been weeping and looked at the Inspector in dazed enquiry. Then she invited him in.

"I'm Mr. Keast's daughter. We don't live here, but I come down to see to mother."

The house had two up and two down. A large room in front and a smaller kitchen behind. There was a bed in one corner of the living-room.

"Mother's been an invalid for years. She can't get upstairs, so we have to have the bed down here."

A pale thin face and two small, almost transparent hands showed over the white counterpane. Bottles of medicine on a side table and a bunch of wildflowers in a pot on the mantelpiece. For the rest, cheap odds and ends of furniture. A few family photographs on the walls and some lustres and an old case-clock on the sideboard. The place was overflowing with furniture, which the bed had packed into one side. A big fire was burning. The room was hot, stuffy and unhealthy.

The old lady lay in her bed like someone in a trance.

"She can't realise it," said her daughter. "She'll not last long now . . . ."

"Is it the Pastor?" asked a feeble voice.

"No, mother, it's a gentleman from the police come enquiring about dad."

"He's a good man, is your dad. I'm sure he'd never do anybody any harm . . . ."

"There, now. Try to sleep, mam. Here, I'll give you your medicine."

"She doesn't understand," said the younger woman, and putting the child down at the foot of the bed, spooned a dose of amber liquid from a bottle into the invalid's mouth.

"He's a good man, is your dad . . . . None better . . . ."

Then the old lady seemed to sleep.

The child wailed feebly and his mother picked him up and dandled him up and down.

"Was you wantin' to know anythin'?"

"Yes. If you don't mind, I'd like to ask you a few questions about your father's movements before his death. Do you know anything about them?"

"Oh, yes. You see, my husband's a porter in the fish-market and doesn't get 'ome to his dinner. So, when I've done my own work, I come down here to look after mam. I leave as a rule about tea-time and then dad comes in to see to her . . . . Or dad *did* . . . "

She started to weep again and had to put the child down. Then she wiped her eyes and nose on her apron and composed herself ready for more talk.

"He was up at the golf club, wasn't he?"

"Yes. Did a bit of caddying, but helped the men with the greens and fairways a lot . . . ."

"Was that all he did?"

"How do you mean?"

"Did he earn anything from other sources?"

"Not that I'd know . . . ."

"Milk!"

"Shhhh. She's asleep."

A farmer hawking milk had put his head round the door. He looked shy at having shouted so loudly.

"How is the old lady?"

"About the same. We tried to tell her about dad, but she can't take it in. So we're just lettin' her be. We's bury him from our place. It 'ud kill her outright to have 'im brought here . . . ."

The man nodded gravely.

"I'm sorry and so is me mother. She told me to tell yer . . . ."

He poured out a couple of pints into a measure and ladled them into a large jug held by the woman.

"If we can do anythin' . . . Good mornin' . . . ."

The woman scratched her untidy hair and looked at Littlejohn for more questions.

"Did your father keep regular hours? I mean had he fixed times for getting home from the links?"

"No. He was later in summer. They play till late."

"Have his habits been regular of late?"

The woman hesitated and then decided to confide.

"No. To tell you the truth. No."

"Tell me about it, please."

"Well . . . Sometimes he's been out all night. He said he'd got to have more money, mam bein' ill for so long. So he took on a job loadin' at the docks. Some of the cargo boats load all night these days. Dad bein' casual labour at the links, like, could get some sleep in the day when he was workin' at night."

"But what about your mother, then?"

"Well . . . My eldest, Norma, is thirteen and came and slept with her grandma when dad was on a job. Not that

I liked it. Dad wasn't gettin' any younger and night work wasn't right at his time o' life. All the same, he was right about mam needin' more money for little luxuries and such. She can't eat everything. It's her inside, you know. Had it nearly all taken away in an operation . . . ."

A little scraggy woman with a string bag put her head in the room.

"I'm just goin' shoppin'. Was you wantin' anything? Not that there's anything much to get. But I thought bein' . . . ."

"Yes, Mrs. Younghusband. Perhaps you'd get a loaf and some tripe if there is any. And maybe a trotter for mam's tea. She likes a trotter now and then . . . ."

"Right. Expect me when you see me, but I'll get 'em if I can. Things is that bad . . . ."

She disappeared as quickly as she had come, nodding sympathetically in the direction of the bed and making sad, clucking noises.

"How often did your father do night work, Mrs . . . . Mrs . . . . ?"

"Mrs. Wright, sir. Oh, one or two nights a week. When one of the Irish boats is in. There's a regular service, you know, between here and Dublin in the summer. General cargo . . . "

"I see. Several boats?"

"Yes."

"Could you tell me please, exactly when, lately, your dad was out at nights, Mrs. Wright?"

The woman wrung her hands and thought.

"Just a minute while I get baby 'is bottle. It's all ready."

She filled an old medicine bottle from a jug warming on the hob, put a rubber teat on the end of it and pushed it in the child's mouth. The child began to suck with great relish . . . .

"I can remember, you see, from when our Norma came to sleep with grandma. It's been Tuesdays and Fridays these last three weeks, I do know that . . . ."

"Thanks very much, Mrs. Wright, and now I'll not trouble you any more . . . ."

"No trouble, sir. I 'ope you'll soon find out who . . . who . . . "

And remembering her bereavement again, she started to weep.

The figure in the bed stirred and spoke feebly.

"'as your dad come 'ome yet, Lottie?"

Down at the dock office they didn't need to look anything up for Littlejohn. They answered pat. The boat in from Ireland on Tuesdays and Fridays was the *Patrick Creegan* of Dublin; master, Isaac Bradley.

The Bishop had been murdered on a Tuesday night at any rate. Had it anything to do with the arrival of the *Patrick Creegan?*

That remained to be seen.

The Customs House was in an old dockside villa and the Chief Officer was tired and near retiring age. Not that there was very much to do at Mervin, but he could do with less.

"Smuggling!" he said to Littlejohn. "Ha, ha, ha. Come again. No, nothing in that line here . . . ."

"But these Irish packets coming in and out just invite it these days . . . ."

Mr. Dunblow, the customs man, was large and round and red and liked rum and a quiet life. He wasn't going to have detectives running him around and telling him how to do his job. He got mad at Littlejohn.

"Look here, if you're insinuatin' that I'm not doing the work here proper, you know who to complain to. I'm fed-up with people, police and the like, nozin' round telling me, whose been on the job forty-two years, how to do it. If they think I'm not doing proper, they know what to do. Pension me off. That's what I'm waitin' for. Pension. Rules, regulations, new contraband, new ways o' gettin' it in, a twopenny-halfpenny port with about three ships comin' and goin' and now you come . . . ."

"Oh, that'll do, Mr. Dunblow. No need to raise the roof. I merely asked for information and I've not got it. I'm much obliged to you for nothing . . . ."

"Smart, ain't you? What do you want to know?"

"How's contraband?"

"As simple as that . . . ."

"Yes, as simple as that."

"Well contraband's quite well, thank you very much. There ain't no smugglin', see . . . ? There ain't none!"

"Very well, as you say, there ain't none. Good day to you, Mr. Dunblow . . . ."

Littlejohn sauntered back to the hotel. He didn't seem to be getting on so fast. From investigations he had a list of possibles in his notebook. He took it out and looked the list over.

Sir Francis Tennant . . . .

Shearwater . . . .

Dr. Mulroy . . . .

One of the Macintosh family . . . .

Nobody else.

A poor lot really. And assuming that one of them had killed the bishop he'd had to take a shot at Littlejohn, fearing he'd found out more than he really had. Next, he'd had to kill Harry Keast, who might have seen too much and be trying blackmail. Sir Francis was unlikely; Shearwater had an alibi; Dr. Mulroy could hardly have known enough to make him shoot Littlejohn; the Macintosh family had just been cleared by a very satisfactory alibi collected by Prickwillow, namely, that the vicar had been there at the time the bishop was killed. The old lady had a mania for backgammon and the vicar sometimes called to play. He had stayed late that night and swore the whole family were there . . . .

So, that was that.

Littlejohn sat on a seat and rested his game leg a bit, Almost before he had settled he was joined by Father O'Shaughnessy.

"Well, Inspector. Feeling better, I hope."

"Yes, thank you, sir. Much better."

"Any nearer a solution of your problem?"

"No, sir. I'm completely stumped. Every little fish that comes in the net manages to get out again."

"Don't say that. You fellows are very good, you know. Rarely fail to get your man, do you?"

The little priest beamed. In one hand he clutched his breviary; in the other his felt hat.

"Let's talk about something else for a bit, sir. I'm tired and could do to take my mind from the problem. Then, perhaps I could come back fresh to it."

"Certainly, what shall we talk about?"

"What part of Ireland are you from, sir?"

"Ballykrushen, a small town in the south. Very sleepy. Nothing much there. Precious few sinners and plenty of time for me to go fishing when I like . . . ."

"Isn't that a bit dead-alive for an active man like you?"

"Not a bit. I like it. It gives me leisure. To tell you the truth, Inspector, I'm a lazy, restless man. If I had a big parish or activities like say the local priest of this town, I'd suffer. I like to travel and read my books. I can do it in my quiet parish. I don't spend all my leisure being lazy in resorts like this. I'm interested in the world around. I've travelled a lot on the Continent and places . . . ."

"Yes, I like travel, too, sir. Been on the Continent a time or two. My wife's a great globe-trotter. You two ought to get together and swap yarns."

"We will, we will, Inspector. What parts of Europe have you seen?"

"Paris, Riviera, Brittany, Switzerland, Rome . . . ."

"So you've been to Rome, have you, Inspector? I like Rome."

"Naturally, you'll like it, father . . . ."

"Yes, but apart from that . . . "

"A lot going on there, I agree. The most interesting thing I ever saw there, I think, was the swearing-in of the Swiss Guard at the Vatican. A great ceremony . . . ."

"Yes, yes. I've seen it, too, when I've been there. Marvellous."

"We happened to be there in the middle of August once, just in time for the swearing-in. They swore-in six new members with great pomp . . . ."

"I've seen it. Magnificent."

"Wonder how things are now in Rome . . . ."

Still chatting they rose and walked back to the hotel.

Fennick, the night porter, had been off duty the night before and having had a full quota of sleep had been up to the hotel for a drink at the bar. He liked doing that. Swanking on his day off and taking a sort of busman's holiday to show that his time was his own.

"I want you, Fennick," said Littlejohn.

"I ain't on duty. My night and day off, see?"

"I just want a word with you . . . ."

"It's my dinner time . . . ."

"Come here. Just tell me this. What's your routine for cleaning shoes at night?"

Fennick looked a bit sheepish.

"Why?"

"Just answer the question. This is police business and it's important."

"Well . . . They's two floors, see? Top floor, I collects the boots as they's put out . . . ."

He didn't say that he did it because the manager slept up there and might catch him cleaning them outside the rooms on the carpet.

" . . . bottom floor, well . . . I cleans 'em outside the doors when all's quiet. Puts paper down to preserve the carpet, like. But you see how it is, sir. I'm gettin' an old man. I can't be up and down stairs like a two-year-old now, can I?"

"No. Is that all Fennick?"

"Yes, sir."

"Right. Thanks very much. What time do you usually collect shoes from the top floor?"

"Well . . . They're usually in their rooms about eleven. About eleven. Then if they's an odd pair out when I takes the clean 'uns back, I does 'em up there."

"Are you a Catholic, Fennick?"

"Yes, sir. Why? That ain't going to 'ave anythin' to do with the murder, is it?"

"No, no. Who's your parish priest?"

"Father Walsh . . . ."

"Is he on the 'phone?"

"Yuss. At the presbytery."

"Very good. That'll be all thanks, Fennick."

Fennick shuffled off muttering to himself. "Priest? Catherlick? The man's barmy . . . ."

"Father Walsh," said Littlejohn to himself and made for the telephone box.

Chapter Sixteen
The Sailor Who Squinted

LITTLEJOHN filled his after-dinner pipe and walked down to the quay. The tide was out and it was dark. There were a few bright lamps along the quayside, but at the far end where the *Patrick Creegan* was moored you only had the masthead lights of the ships and the glow of the lamps over the fo'c'sles to guide you. You had to step carefully to avoid the ropes coiled round the bollards.

The ships were low in the water, funnels and masts only visible. Here and there footsteps shambled on decks. One of the trawlers was getting-up steam and smoke poured from its funnel across the harbour. There was a sailor leaning over the side . . . .

"Which is the *Patrick Creegan?*"

"Tied up at the far end there . . . ."

"When does she sail?"

"First thing to-morrow . . . . She's just waiting for the tide . . . ."

Littlejohn crossed the gang plank. It was quiet on deck, but there was somebody below in the fo'c'sle. Subdued voices and someone softly playing a mouth-organ. A light shone through the porthole of the small cabin below the bridge. Littlejohn's footsteps echoed as he walked about. He knocked at the door of the captain's cabin.

"Come in . . . ."

The place was small and simply furnished. A bunk covered with a dirty rug faced you as you entered. The lower part was a chest of drawers. Two wall-cupboards, a washstand which folded into the wall, and a hinged table which let down when not in use. There was the remains of a meal on the table, which was covered with a black American-leather cloth.

Captain Bradley was sitting reading the paper with his feet on the table. Tall and lean, big nose slightly askew, heavy jaw and loose lips. His arms and legs were abnormally long. He needed a shave.

But the thing you noticed first was his eyes. Close set and out of true. One looked straight at you; the other squinted badly.

"Well . . . "

Littlejohn obviously wasn't welcome.

Captain Bradley put down his paper. He'd been filling-in a penny pool. Littlejohn introduced himself and sat down without being invited on a chair clamped to the floor behind the door.

"Well, what do you want? I don't see how I come to be mixed-up in the case just because the fellow happened to be a casual loading hand . . . ."

There was just a trace of brogue in the speech; otherwise he mightn't have been Irish at all. The sort of man you find hanging round third-rate ships and who, in times of depression, can't get a master's job and has to take second or third, unless he's on something shady . . . .

"You more or less make regular trips between here and Ireland . . . ?"

"Yes. What's that to do with it?"

"Dublin?"

"Yes . . . ."

"What do you carry . . . ?"

"Cattle mostly, but what's all this to do with Harry Keast?"

"Do you know, Captain Bradley, I've an idea Harry Keast had something to tell me about what goes on on board this ship and for that he lost his life."

"Look here. I was in Eire at home when Harry Keast was killed. I'd nothing to do with it. So don't you be trying to mix me in this murder business."

"Who owns this vessel?"

"The Dublin and Mervin Steamship Company. Why?"

"Is she registered here?"

"Go to hell . . . . You can find that out from the port authorities, or you can see from her stern who she is and where she comes from . . . ."

"She's registered here, I believe."

"Then why ask me?"

"Just making conversation . . . ."

"Look here, mister, you're wasting my time. We sail with the tide and we've a lot to do. So, detective or no detective, scram . . . ."

With his squint and his crooked nose, Captain Bradley looked an ugly customer and his temper had not been improved by the rum he'd been drinking. The place reeked of it. He picked up a cigarette from a packet on the table and lit it without offering Littlejohn one.

"Guess you find those cheap in your job . . . ."

"What are you getting at?"

"Cigarettes, silk stockings and the like come cheaply in Eire, I hear, and with a customs officer like Dunblow, I guess it shouldn't be difficult . . . ."

The look Bradley gave Littlejohn was positively revolting.

"I don't take that from anybody, see? I've a good record and a clean ticket and this ship's got a good reputation . . . ."

He uncurled his legs and stood up, his long arms dangling like those of a great ape. He was a good two inches taller than Littlejohn and wiry and strong with it.

"Well, mister? Are you going? Or do I put you off the ship?"

"I'll go under my own steam, thank you. But I'll be back one day, Captain Bradley. Good night . . . ."

Bradley slammed the door.

The boat smelled of pitch, cattle and fish.

The man with the mouth-organ was leaning over the side playing softly to himself. He did it like a professional, fanning the instrument with one hand and sliding it about with the other. *William Tell.* He must have fancied himself on the halls one day . . . .

"What are you carrying this time . . . ?"

The man stopped the *Gallop* and wiped the moisture from the mouthpiece. You couldn't make out what he looked like, except that he was fairly tall. Just a paleness for a face, and fluttering hands . . . .

"Coal . . . "

"Not very big, is she?"

"No. Crew of five and the captain. A pig in rough weather . . . "

"What'll you be bringing back?"

"Cattle, I guess. Messy game, specially when its stormy . . . ."

"Cattle . . . and the rest, eh?"

"*And* the rest . . . Here . . . What you gettin' at?"

He had been so busy thinking of his music that he'd spoken too quickly. He suddenly realised that he was being quizzed.

Littlejohn didn't press the matter. He left the man tuning-up again and made for his hotel.

It was getting late, but there was still a lot to do.

Bowater was waiting for Littlejohn in the small deserted smokeroom. The place was so old-fashioned and uncomfortable that nobody ever used it. They preferred the bar. The Superintendent was standing with his back to the fire. He had been there half an hour and someone had put a match to the sticks and paper, which burned as though undecided whether or not to give up the ghost.

Bowater didn't seem to mind being kept waiting. The business in hand seemed to worry him more.

"I don't know what good it'll do, but I've got them for you."

He produced a snapshot showing Shearwater and Father O'Shaughnessy walking along the promenade. The priest was holding his hat on but hadn't hidden his face.

"Our man did the usual trick. Snapped them and gave them a ticket, numbered, advising them the photos would be ready at the address given to-morrow morning, price one and six each. The address was a genuine studio, just in case . . . "

"This is very good . . . I'm glad. Now send one to the Dublin police and the other to Scotland Yard. Did your man manage to get the fingerprints?"

"Yes . . . They'd been playing billiards and he collared their glasses from the waiter . . . ."

"Get going on those, too, will you?"

"Where's all this leading?"

"I don't quite know, but I'd like to find out if that pair have any criminal records. By the way, have you seen Father Walsh about?"

"Yes. Saw him going in the Allains' private room. He calls on them sometimes, I believe. They belong to his church."

"So I gather. I asked him to call . . . "

"Whatever for?"

"Let's try to find him and we'll see."

On the way they passed the lounge. The gamblers were still playing busily in their usual place in the window. Hennessy looked bored to death. Only Rooksby seemed to be concentrating on the game. Sharples kept looking nervously around and Wentworth was almost asleep. Sharples spotted Littlejohn and said something to the rest . . . .

"By the way, Bowater, is that gambling gang interested in the Dublin and Mervin Steamship Company?"

"Yes . . . Hennessy's chairman and the rest hold shares, I think. Why?"

"I was just wondering . . . ."

Bowater seemed to take it for granted that the questions were leading somewhere. He didn't know where, but was too bewildered to pursue the matter.

Father Walsh was sitting with the proprietor in his private room. A small, stocky man with a rugged face and a pleasant smile. Very popular with his flock, especially the children. He had a glass of brandy at his elbow. It was a balloon-glass and you could tell by the way he handled it that he appreciated a good thing when he got it.

"Well, father . . . ?"

The priest looked up and smiled. He warmed his glass in the palms of his hands.

"O'Shaughnessy's a funny priest. Allain pretended to introduce him to me just fortuitously. We had a little talk. I'm Irish, too, you see. He knows quite a lot about Ireland, but he doesn't know much Latin. I searched him out a bit . . . I think he's masquerading as a priest . . . ."

"So I thought . . . ."

"Why?"

"I didn't quite know how you set about finding out whether a priest is genuine or not, but as he'd been to Rome, he said, and knew all about the Vatican, I tried him on the only test I knew. He never corrected me when I told him I'd seen all the pomp and ceremony of six Swiss Guards being sworn-in in August . . . ."

Father Walsh threw back his head and roared.

"Very good, Inspector. Very good . . . ."

"They never swear in less than ten publicly and never in August . . . ."

"That's right. I call that smart of you . . . ."

"Well, O'Shaughnessy's such a know-all, he'd never have failed to correct me if he'd known the true facts, which he ought to have done . . . "

Allain looked very disturbed.

"I hope I'm not housing a nest of thieves here, Inspector."

"No, no, sir. Nothing may come of it. O'Shaughnessy may simply have nothing to do with the present case at all, but we'll have to make quite sure of that . . . . By the way, father, have you heard of a place called Ballykrushen in Eire?"

"No. Why?"

"O'Shaughnessy's supposed to be parish priest there . . . ."

"No. I guess it's like him. A fake . . . ."

"We'll find out. Perhaps you'll do that for us, Superintendent . . . ."

Bowater nodded. He, too, was busy with a balloon-glass, but didn't quite know what it was all about. He gazed in bewilderment at the large vessel and the small drop of brandy in the bottom of it . . . .

Cromwell's face appeared at the glass door. He had an earnest questing look on it, which turned to triumph when he spotted Littlejohn. He knocked and entered.

"Can you spare a minute, sir . . . ."

"Yes, Cromwell. What is it? You can tell me here . . . ."

"I've been enquiring the movements of Shearwater and the priest on the afternoon you were shot. They went off for the day in Shearwater's car. A day's pleasure excursion, I believe . . . ."

"These two always seem to be together, don't they? Especially when an alibi's wanted. Are they in the bar?"

"The priest is . . . . Shearwater's not there . . . ."

"How did you get the information . . . ?"

"From the head-waiter. They had to tell him with not being back for lunch."

"I see. A good idea asking the head-waiter. Anybody who stayed here for lunch couldn't have taken a pot at me. Too far away. Did you enquire about any of the others?"

"Yes. The doctor . . . Rooksby, wasn't in. But it was near his consulting time and he always has lunch in his rooms then. The other three dined-in."

"You checked Rooksby?"

"Yes. I rang up his secretary pretending I'd forgotten an appointment that day and asking if it was all right. She said my name wasn't down and that things had gone on normally. It would appear he was on duty then."

"Yes. Anybody else?"

"Sir Francis Tennant was out for the day fishing. Went off alone early in the morning and didn't get back till late . . . ."

"Oh. Let's see the priest and Shearwater then, before they go to bed . . . ."

Father O'Shaughnessy was just emerging jovially from the bar. He halted to wish Littlejohn good night.

"You remember the day somebody shot at me, father? I believe you and Mr. Shearwater were out on an excursion . . . Now, you needn't answer if you don't want, but as I'm checking up everywhere, perhaps you'd help me . . . ."

"You don't mean to tell me I'm suspect of firing a rifle at you, do you, Inspector? My dear fellow, I think far too much of you for that . . . ."

"I know, father, but . . . "

"Of course, Inspector, I don't want to break your usual routine. We went to Faithness to look at the lighthouse and had lunch there. And returned by Cleary Glen and Ruston Caves. We'd tea at a café near the caves and lunch we took as sandwiches provided by our friend the head-waiter."

"Did you go in the lighthouse?"

"I'm afraid not, Inspector. There were a lot of charabanc parties there and the place was so busy. We sat on the shingle for a time. It was hot and pleasant and we enjoyed the scene. So, as usual, Shearwater and I are one another's alibis, unless, of course, you care to track down the charabanc parties. We spoke to several members, but I expect by this time they'll all be home with holidays almost forgotten."

"Let's see Mr. Shearwater, too, just to confirm that, father. Not that I doubt a word you say, but his account will be taken in any case."

"He's gone to bed, Inspector. He seemed very tired, so after a drink in the bar, he retired. Abount three-quarters of an hour ago, that would be."

"Right, I'll see him in the morning. Thank you, father, and good night."

Fennick was on duty and pottering about the hall waiting for time to collect his shoes and settle down for the night.

"Just get Mr. Shearwater's shoes for me, please, Fennick, will you?"

The porter's eyes almost dropped from his head.

"But . . . "

"Just do as I ask, please. It's important."

Fennick patted his wig and went off. He was soon back.

"He ain't put out his shoes and he ain't in his room, as far as I can 'ear."

Littlejohn hurried upstairs as fast as his game leg would allow, Cromwell following and sympathetically moderating his pace with his chief's.

There was nobody in Shearwater's room and his hand-luggage had gone, too. It looked very much as if he had bolted.

Chapter Seventeen
The Departure of the "Patrick Greegan"

MRS. MACINTOSH was in bed when Littlejohn telephoned her at Greyle, but they brought her to speak to him.

She sounded tired and afraid.

"You knew your brother was staying at the hotel here at the same time as you and your late husband, Mrs. Macintosh?"

"Er . . . er . . . "

"He's already told me you met, so you need have no fear . . . ."

"Yes, I met him, but we kept the meeting quiet. I didn't want my husband to know. He'd have been very upset."

"Well, madam, your brother has just disappeared . . . ."

There was a gasp at the other end.

"Did you know his London address? It may be that he has gone back there without telling anyone."

"Yes. We kept in touch. We were very attached to one another in times past. But I didn't let the bishop know. He wasn't fond of my brother."

"Can you give me the address, please? It's imperative that I get hold of him."

"He's not going to be arrested for anything, is he?"

"No. But maybe his life is in danger. I must find him. Please hurry."

"He lodges with an old servant of the family. Mrs. Greer, 13, Benson's Mews, off Eaton Square. I do hope you find him . . . ."

Littlejohn telephoned Scotland Yard at once to send a man along to watch Benson's Mews. Shearwater had not yet had time to reach London. Driving at his fastest, his car wouldn't make it for another two hours. Police patrols were warned to be on the look-out.

The young detective detailed to keep an eye on the watchman on the quay turned-in with a negative report. The man he was watching had done nothing all night except tend his lamps and ruminate over his fire.

"Bring him in to the police station. Perhaps there he'll talk better than in the hotel. I'll come along with you, Bowater, and we'll see him together. Meanwhile, I want your man to stay here and report if Father O'Shaughnessy leaves . . . ."

The priest had gone to bed quite unperturbed by his friend's disappearance, but it was as well to keep an eye on him in view of Father Walsh's opinion about him.

The watchman was furious at being brought away from his fire and his lamps at that time of night.

"What's the use of bein' a watchman if you're not there to watch?" he asked.

But he was more impressed and subdued by the charge-room at the police station than he was at the hotel. Furthermore, he'd had a few drinks and was a bit sorry for himself.

"A policeman's keeping an eye on your pitch whilst you're away, Jeale, so you needn't worry," said Bowater. "And by the way, haven't you and I met before? Let me see, what was it? Yes . . . Drunk and disorderly and assaulting an officer . . . ."

"You can't bring that up against me. Miscarriage o' justice, that's what it was. The bobby hit me first . . . ."

"We won't discuss that now, Jeale. What we want to know is, what comings and goings after eleven have you to report over the last few days, say the night the bishop was killed,—remember it?—and since . . . "

Jeale wasn't comfortable at all. Whether or not he'd seen people passing at the stated times, he certainly had something on his conscience.

"I seen nothin' important, as I told him before. Courtin' couples and the like . . . ."

Littlejohn intervened.

"How long have you been on that job, Jeale?"

"Nearly twelve months."

"What did you do before?"

"Labouring on the docks . . . ."

"Casual?"

"Yes."

"Who found you this work?"

"The Corporation, of course. They're doin' the job."

"Have they been at it nearly a year?"

"Yes. But had to leave it for a while on account of the men makin' roads for the new housin' scheme."

"Seems funny to me having a watchman there all that time if the job's in abeyance."

"Nothin' to do with me. I gets my pay and I'm satisfied."

"Who in the Corporation got you the job?"

"Borough Surveyor's Department. Under the Highways Committee."

"Who on the committee recommended you?"

Jeale paused and sucked his gums.

"Come on now, Jeale. No stalling any longer. If you've got information you'd best tell us. This murder business will soon be cleared-up now and I hope you're not going to be mixed-up in the end of it."

The policemen were locking up a drunk in one of the cells. He was shouting the place down.

"Shut that door and stop that row . . . ."

Bowater's temper was frayed. The case was getting on his nerves.

"I ain't done nothin' about the murder. I swear it. All I can tell you is Councillor Sharples got me the job . . . ."

"Sharples. Is that the little man who plays cards at the hotel?"

"Yes," said Bowater. "But I don't see what all this has to do . . . "

"Wait a minute. Are you doing anything for Councillor Sharples now, Jeale? I mean casual work or something in exchange for the job he got you?"

Jeale was properly scared. He kept looking at the door as though getting ready to make a run for it.

"Come on now, or I'll lock you up till morning . . . ."

Bowater looked ready to punch Jeale's head for prevaricating.

"If you do, your man'll be on my job all night, that's all, and I'll be cosy here. So that'll not do much good."

"All the same, Jeale, you look as though you're set on being mixed-up in all this dirty work. Very well, if you want it that way . . . ."

Littlejohn waved a hand towards the door. This time, Jeale didn't seem interested in getting away. He was deciding what he had to say and how to say it.

"It's this way. Mr. Sharples asked me to say nothing about it if I wanted to keep the job, but I do him a favour now and then which doesn't matter a cuss to anybody but him . . . ."

"Well?"

"Well . . . He's the main man of the Dublin and Mervin boats and says the harbour lights here are poor. While we have the lamps on the quayside job, there's two of them right at the end can be seen from the sea, he tells me. Well, at certain times to help navigatin' his ships, he says the lights on my pitch'll help his captains. On some nights a red on the left and a white on the right, shows the state o' the tide, and on others a white on the left and a white on the right, shows another tide. He was to tell me when which was which. He's only told me twice, so I haven't done much to earn my job yet."

"I see. Well, you're not to tell a soul you've told us this. Understand?"

"Course I do. Think I'll go blabbin' when me job depends on it?"

"And another thing. Tell me whenever you get one of those messages from Councillor Sharples. I'm very interested in the tides here, Jeale. And now you can go, thanks."

"Red lights and white lights. It all sounds daft to me," said Bowater.

"Not so daft as you'd think. We'll soon see?"

Outside the night was clear and starry. The *Patrick Creegan* was still tied-up at the pierhead as Littlejohn made his way back to the hotel. The men on board were busy getting ready to cast-off. No sign of Captain Bradley, however.

"Any passengers this trip?" asked Littlejohn of one of the men.

"No, guv'nor. This ain't much of a luxury liner. Specially in rough weather."

"When you due back?"

"Night after to-morrow . . . ."

Suddenly the door of the captain's little cabin opened and Bradley came out, climbed the little iron ladder and stood on the bridge.

He didn't issue any explicit orders.

"Right . . . "

The hawsers were slipped from the bollards, the engine-room telegraph clanged and in a few minutes the *Patrick Creegan* was gently gliding into the middle of the river. The screw began to revolve faster, and she quietly slipped out to sea . . . .

There was still a light in the customs-house. Littlejohn tapped on the door and somebody unlocked it.

"Hullo. What you after at this time o' night?"

It wasn't Dunblow but a young fellow with a fresh, humorous face.

"You keep late hours. May I come in a minute?"

"These aren't official hours, you know. I've been out with my girl and left my overcoat here while we went to the pictures. I've just called for it. Another minute and the place would have been in darkness . . . ."

"What's your job here?"

The young chap didn't seem to mind being quizzed, but kept smiling patiently. He must have had a good time with his girl at the pictures.

"Im third man here. Mr. Dunblow, Mr. Medlicott, and then me. Who are you, by the way?"

"I'm the man from Scotland Yard investigating the death of the Bishop of Greyle . . . ."

"Oh, I've heard of you. But surely we've nothing to do with that down here."

"I don't know. What do you think of Mr. Dunblow, if it's a fair question?"

"Between you and me, not so much. He's panting for retirement and very fed-up and disappointed that he's not got on faster to get a bigger pension. A bit slack now, you know. Things'll be tightened up when he goes, I'll tell you. Mr. Medlicott'll stand no messin'."

"Very efficient?"

"I'll say. Mind you, I won't say Mr. Dunblow would do anything wrong. But at a job like this, if you're slack, people get to know and take advantage. There's not much shipping here luckily, but if Dunblow and Medlicott were on duty at say, Holyhead or Dover, I know when I'd try smuggling-in Swiss watches or French wines."

"Oh, it's that way, is it?"

"Yes."

"What time do you open in a morning?"

"Eight."

"And close?"

"Normally around five. If there's a boat comes in at a reasonable hour, we might clear her before we go, even if it is a bit late, but, as a rule, when the night boats come in, they've to tie-up and wait till we come on duty."

"I guess that happens with the *Patrick Creegan,* too."

"Yes. With all of them."

"And suppose a boat came in when you were off duty and anybody tried to get ashore with contraband . . . ?"

"That's not allowed till we've cleared them. The dock police would stop any monkey-work."

"Well, I guess you're wanting to be off. Good-night and thanks for the help."

"I can't see how that helps to solve the bishop's murder. However, you know better than me. Good night, sir."

Littlejohn paused at the door.

"By the way, have you a rota of duties?"

"Yes. Why?"

"Who was in charge on the day the bishop's body was found at Bolter's Hole?"

"What date would that be . . . ? Never mind. It doesn't matter. It would be Mr. Dunblow. Mr. Medlicott's been away nearly three weeks on holidays with his family. Dunblow's been like a bear with a sore ear. He doesn't like holidays. Bring him extra duties, such as they are . . . ."

At the hotel, Fennick was in his den, having cleaned all his shoes and banked-up his fires for the night. Spread before him on the table were his football pool sheets in all their glory and, scattered around, the sporting pages of several papers from which the poller was taking his pick and laboriously marking his forms. He hastily put on his abandoned wig and faced Littlejohn as the Inspector knocked on the open door.

"You're up late, sir . . . ."

Fennick spoke resentfully. It meant that he would have to trail up for Littlejohn's shoes and clean them after the Inspector had retired for the night. It wasn't fair. Took a man's mind off his more important other duties, trying to earn enough in prize money to be able to snap his fingers at the boss and leave all the shoes dirty for a change.

"Did you get hold of Father O'Shaughnessy's shoes for me, Fennick?"

"Yes, sir. And took 'em back again, too. Thought you'd forgotten about them."

"Please get them again."

Fennick smothered his annoyance and slowly emerged from his lair, crawled upstairs, crawled down again and placed a pair of clean, well-worn shoes on the table before Littlejohn.

"There . . . "

Littlejohn examined the shoes, handed them back to Fennick with a shilling, bade him good night and went off to bed.

Fennick spat on the coin and stuffed it in his pocket, spat on the shoes for luck, took them back upstairs and then returned to finish chasing a fortune.

He wasn't undisturbed for long. The buzzer on the switchboard suddenly broke the silence.

"'ullo. Yuss. Wot, at this hour? Righto, wait a bit. I'll 'ave to get him."

Cursing under his breath the porter plugged the line through to Littlejohn's room.

Shearwater had turned-up at Benson's Mews, had been briefly interrogated, and told not to leave. An officer had remained there on guard.

"I'll be along in the morning, then. I'm *supposed* to be on holiday and I'm dying for a night's sleep. So keep him under observation and hold him if necessary till I arrive. Good night."

With that, Littlejohn went back to bed.

Chapter Eighteen
Benson's Mews

FATHER O'SHAUGHNESSY met Littlejohn at breakfast the following morning. He was his usual bland, fresh self, but there was an anxious look in his eyes.

"Have you heard anything more of Shearwater?" he asked.

"No," answered Littlejohn, returning smile for smile. "He's a bit of a mystery, you know. Been abroad, changed his name and one thing and another. I've no idea why he's run out or where to. I'm anxious that he shouldn't go, however, till this case is settled. After all, we want to keep as many as possible of those who were here at the time of the murder about us. You, in particular, have your alibis in Shearwater. Not that I suggest for a moment, father . . . "

"No, no. Of course not. What are you doing to-day?"

"I'm going to Scotland Yard to clear up some arrears which I left before I came here. I'm really due back now, but my accident, of course . . . I hope to return to-night after a conference."

"We shall see you again, then?"

"Probably at dinner."

The sergeant in charge of the tracing of Shearwater met Littlejohn in Eaton Square, and together they drove to Benson's Mews.

"We've watched the front, sir," the sergeant told him. "There's a small yard at the back, but no way out, unless he climbs a high wall and then he'd have to come out into the mews. These places were constructed from old stables, you see."

Littlejohn knocked at the door which was opened by a tall, thin woman dressed in black. Her front teeth projected, she had wispy grey hair and her bust was laced high and tight in corsets, the outlines of which showed through her silk blouse.

Shearwater was sitting in the kitchen in an old basket-chair. The room lay at the end of a long corridor from which two other doors led to furnished bed-sitting rooms. The doors were open showing unmade beds with the sheets and blankets draping their ends. On the floor, empty ewers and slop-pails ready for carrying away . . . .

The back room was dark, for the light from the sash window was dimmed by the walls of a narrow yard which hung over it. The place was hot and smelled of cooking. A large table in the middle, odds and ends of chairs round it, two or three framed pictures from Christmas almanacs on the walls. Littlejohn could make out The Meeting of Dante and Beatrice . . . .

Shearwater seemed to be waiting patiently. He looked relieved when Littlejohn entered.

"I was thinking of coming back," he said. "It was foolish of me to run off . . . ."

"Why did you do it?"

"I got a bit scared."

"What of?"

"I don't know, really. The death of Harry Keast was a shock to me. I thought that I might be next."

"Why?"

The old lady was pottering about in the room. Clattering dishes in the sink, fiddling about with the gas stove, taking things up and putting them down again. All the time with one ear in the direction of the conversation. She was evidently fond of Shearwater and kept casting an anxious eye in his direction whilst glaring malevolently at Littlejohn.

"All right, Bridget. You'd better leave us, please."

The woman sniffed, marched out and banged the door. You could hear her rattling the slop pails in the bedrooms and stamping about the floors.

"Why?"

Shearwater paused. He seemed undecided whether or not to tell Littlejohn everything. The Inspector had an idea what was coming but did not press him.

"You see, I've rather foolishly acted as alibi to Father O'Shaughnessy."

"Well, weren't you with him when you said you were?"

"Sometimes. It's this way. O'Shaughnessy fancied himself as an amateur detective. He wanted to investigate the bishop's murder without your knowing. He told me that before it happened he suspected something funny afoot in the hotel and at Bolter's Hole and wanted to find the solution first . . . ."

"Excuse me, Mr. Shearwater, let's get this clear. Did he tell you this before or after the crime?"

"After. He told me after that he was doing a bit of quiet sleuthing before the murder. He asked me not to tell you, and to cover his investigations in certain places he got me to give him alibis."

"That was criminally foolish of you, sir. But go on. Give me details of these alibis, please."

"Well, I admit I had drunk a bit too much on the night the bishop died. I'm afraid Father O'Shaughnessy rather encouraged me, too. We played billiards and he kept ordering drinks. He saw me to bed and then went out of my room right away, to go to bed himself, he said."

"Yes, I guess he did go to bed and whilst in his room, he had his shoes gathered-in by the hallporter. So he borrowed Mr. Cuhady's . . . ."

Even under the tension of the moment, both men smiled at the recollection of Cuhady and his footwear.

"Go on . . . ."

"When you were shot, O'Shaughnessy and I weren't far away. He said he wanted to follow you to pick up any threads you might have gathered that he didn't know. We saw you go to Cranage Farm. Then the priest parked the car, or told me to do so,—it was my car,—and left me eating sandwiches whilst he went for a walk round. He was away quite a while."

"Had he a rifle with him?"

"No. That's how I knew he couldn't have shot you. A bit weak of me covering him the way I did, but I thought I was being a sport joining him in the hunt."

"I see . . . . Just excuse me a minute."

Littlejohn went out to where he had left the detective-sergeant in the police car.

"Just ring up the police station at Medhope, near Greyle, and ask for Constable Prickwillow. If he's not in, tell somebody to give him this message. I want him to check all the rifles, the .44s licensed between Cranage Farm and Medhope, find if any one is missing and get to know why. To be reported to me per Port Mervin police station as soon as possible. Full details, please."

"Very good, sir . . . ."

The old woman was in the kitchen again whispering to Shearwater when Littlejohn got back. They had to send her out.

"I was only seeing about a cup of tea," she grumbled.

"To resume, sir. Were you actually with the priest when Harry Keast was shot?"

"No. I was sitting on the seat by the tee near Bolter's Hole and O'Shaughnessy was scrambling about, actually in the Hole. The tide was out and he said he wanted to see the spot where the bishop died."

"You saw Keast fall?"

"Yes. The shot sounded like a snapping twig or something. I saw Keast sag down and thought he'd had a fit. The next was, the priest was running to him and calling me to help."

"Didn't it dawn on you that O'Shaughnessy might have shot Keast?"

"Not till the other night. Then putting two and two together, I got scared. But him being a priest, it seemed impossible. All the same, I impulsively bolted, called here for my trunk and was met by your man, who told me to stay put. In any case, I ought to have come to you at once and I'd made up my mind to return and tell you when your man arrived."

"Would it surprise you to learn that he's not a priest at all?"

Shearwater took it quite calmly.

"No, not now. He looks like one and behaved like one until Keast died. But looking back on events last night, I suddenly remembered how he acted with Keast's dead body. He hadn't somehow the priestly touch in the face of death. They generally do something reverent. Either composing the limbs, crossing themselves, praying or something. But he was too business-like. I don't know . . . The thing seemed wrong instinctively."

"I understand. So the alibis are washed out and O'Shaughnessy's conduct throughout is highly suspicious."

"Yes. I'm sorry to have caused you all this trouble. I'm ready to take my medicine. I guess I've to pay for my stupidity.

But I want you to know I didn't kill my brother-in-law, or Keast, or take a pot at you."

"I believe you, sir. And now, I need your help badly. I've a plan I want to put into action and you're a vital part in it. So vital, that unless you co-operate, O'Shaughnessy may slip through our fingers. As to your running out on us, it may turn out to have been the most fortunate move. You might have guessed rightly, too, that you would be the next victim."

"What do you want me to do?"

The old woman came worrying in again.

"Did you want a cup of tea, Mr. Rupert?"

She ignored Littlejohn.

"Yes, Bridget, if you please. It wouldn't come amiss. Make one for the Inspector, too."

The woman grunted and put the kettle on.

Shearwater stood up. He hadn't had a shave and looked haggard from being up all night, but there was a new composure about his features, as though he'd eased his mind by making the right decision.

"That priest surely led me up the garden path. I'm glad of a chance to get even with him."

The lid of the kettle began to dance and steam puffed from the spout. The old woman rushed in and got busy with the tea things.

"One question, Mr. Shearwater. Had you any knowledge of a smuggling racket going on at Cape Mervin?"

"No. Is there one?"

"I suspect so. Something pretty big. What made you settle there?"

"As a matter of fact, I met an old friend, Sir Francis Tennant. You'll perhaps have seen him at the hotel. A retired judge. I met him dining in the West End one night and we had a long talk. I was worn-out in London after all my travels and I haven't been well for some time. It seems Tennant goes down to Mervin quite a lot fishing. He recommended me to try it and said he'd see they made me comfortable. It was quiet, too, he said. Looking back, I think he did it deliberately to get me to meet my sister again. Frank was always in love with Evelyn and knowing how fond she and I were of each other, maybe he did her one of his usual good turns. Her getting married to a rival never seemed to stop his looking after her. I was surprised when Evelyn and her husband turned-up, and we were both so glad to meet again."

"So that was it. What a mix-up you got into. I suppose you met O'Shaughnessy soon after you arrived."

"Yes. He tacked himself on to me. I always thought he was too good a billiards player for a parson. Still, you never know, do you?"

"He was looking out for some kind friend to be his alibi and picked on you."

"Yes. I was his stooge, it seems. What do you want me to do?"

Over teacups Littlejohn explained his plan.

"The thing now is to get back to Cape Mervin?"

"Yes. And on the way we'll call at Scotland Yard and you can sign a statement of all you've told me. You'll not come out of this so badly, if you do as I say, sir."

"Thank you, Inspector. Shall we go, then?"

The old woman cried when they left and, kissing Shearwater, told him there was always a home there for him. Then she wiped her eyes and blew her nose on the corner of her apron and went back to wash-up the dirty cups.

Chapter Nineteen
The Return of the "Patrick Creegan"

JEALE, the night-watchman, had received a message from Sharples to put a white light on the left and a white on the right. It was unusual but he'd better let the police know to keep himself out of trouble. Difficult serving two masters, but when one of them is the police . . . well . . . He spat on his hands and rubbed them up and down his corduroy trousers as he always did when he had something on his mind or was going to start a drunken brawl or argument. He shambled to the telephone box near his pitch, dialled 'O' and asked for the police station.

"You should have dialled 999," said the instrument.

"Gimme the pleece and don't argue. This is special . . . ."

The next minute he was speaking to Bowater.

"Leave them as they usually are. One red, one white," came the reply to the long rigmarole Jeale spoke into the telephone. He hadn't done much telephoning in his life and was impressed by the ease with which he did it and the wonder of it all. He talked a lot about it at the local when he was half seas over the following night.

The *Patrick Creegan* came in on the next tide with more men aboard than she was accustomed to carry.

Earlier that night Captain Bradley looked from the bridge with his night glasses and was surprised to see the usual signal.

"Either they've led off that damned detective or else the boss is taking a hell of a risk. Anyhow the signal's there, so get crackin'."

The mate gave gruff orders and the small crew set to work. There was some cattle on board but for the most part the cargo consisted of cases of cigarettes, liquor, stockings, clothing and other stuff, either contraband or else articles you couldn't get without coupons in the normal channels and which consequently had considerably enhanced values in black markets.

The men worked quietly loading the ship's two boats and fixing outboard motors to them. Then they cast-off and steered right between the two lights of Jeale's lamps until the rising coast cut them off. The mate in the first boat quickly flashed his torch three times. Three intermittent pin-points of light from land answered him. This performance was repeated at brief intervals.

The mate steered his craft into Bolter's Hole first, flashed again, received his answer and made for the spot whence it came. The other boat followed close on his stern. The quiet throbbing of motors ceased and they glided in . . . .

"Ahoy there!" growled the mate in a stage whisper.

Then the place seemed to become alive with dark, rushing figures. Police helmets and huge forms grew visible in the gloom.

"Come on there; better keep quiet and behave. There's plenty of us. Oh . . . So it's you, is it? Well . . . well . . . "

The sergeant-in-charge was enjoying himself. He breathed onions over the mate, for he had eaten a good supper before setting out on his night's adventure.

"Lumme," said the mate and gave in without a struggle.

Each man handcuffed to a constable, the three smugglers scrambled without dignity up the sides of Bolter's Hole to terra firma on top. The progress of the police couldn't be described as graceful either. They'd been ordered to show no lights except answer signals, which they hoped to heaven were right, and they did part of the rocky ascent on their hands and knees, hoisting their quarry along willynilly. Other policemen unloaded the boats and carried their loot to a waiting van.

Littlejohn and Bowater watched it all without taking much part but with great satisfaction.

"Well I never," Bowater kept saying in surprise, for Littlejohn himself had not anticipated such a haul in one trip.

The whole of the cargo and men cleared-up, the two officers and two policemen boarded the boats and after starting the motors, steered for the *Patrick Creegan.* On the way they received and answered pin-point signals and soon were alongside the ship. They caught the rope flung out to them and ascended the rope ladder. At this point they almost gave themselves away, for their progress upward was far from nautical.

"What the hell've you been doin'?" growled Captain Bradley by way of greeting. "There's two more loads for you yet. We don't want to be here all night."

"Evening, Bradley," said Littlejohn.

"Well, I'll go to 'ell," replied the Captain, and bolted for the rail. It is not quite certain what he intended to do. Throw himself overboard, or stand and fight with his back to the wall . . . . But he met the outstretched leg of one of the constables first, measured his length with a thud on the deck and threw up the sponge without a fight.

Down in the cabin as they slowly sailed into port, Bradley was very bitter about his employers.

"What the hell do they mean sending the right signal when you swine were about?"

He didn't say swine, but the other word might not be printed.

"We changed the signals."

"*You!* Well, I like that. So somebody gave the show away, did they? I told the boss before we left this trip that you lot were about and he'd better call it off for a bit. He looked wise and said I could rely on him to do the right thing. And now look at us . . . ."

He burst into a torrent of more unprintable words until Bowater got mad and vulgarly told him to shut his trap.

"Who is the boss? Sharples?"

"If you know, why ask me? But I'll get even with the little perisher. Havin' me pullin' his chestnuts out of the fire, while him and his pals sit pretty playing cards. *And* raking-in the dough. I'll spill the beans, blessed if I don't."

He didn't actually say 'blessed,' but then . . .

"Better tell us what happens on these trips and be done with it. It's bound to come out . . . "

"I don't like the rough way I've been handled by you bastards," grumbled Bradley and his language was interrupted this time by the blast of the siren warning the harbourmaster that they were wanting to enter port.

"I'd better get on the bridge . . . ."

They went with him.

But before the gangway was put out, the police had another talk with Bradley. It was as they had guessed. After leaving Dublin they made for a quiet spot and took on contraband and other stuff made ready by an agent in Eire. Then they made the crossing, unloaded the stuff at Bolter's Hole, where it was met by men who carried it by hand to Sharples's hiding-place, the cellars of a large house turned into a warehouse on the quay. The red and white lights ashore told that the coast was clear. Two white lights warned them to dump the stuff over the side. Better be rid of it than have it confiscated and the whole arrangement be ruined. They'd only needed to do that once, when an old fool of a parson turned up at Bolter's Hole and recognised Harry Keast . . . ."

"Harry Keast?"

"Yes. Harry was in charge of the gang of porters who carried the stuff to town."

"I guessed something of that kind," said Littlejohn. "Who killed the parson?"

"I don't know. That was very hush-hush. They said it was an accident."

"Accident my foot. He was deliberately decoyed to Bolter's Hole and murdered."

"You seem to know all about it. Suppose you do the tellin' and let me listen a bit . . . ."

"That'll do. What do you know about the parson, Bradley?"

"Only this. Harry Keast told me the fellow got to takin' a walk across to the Hole at nights, late on, to meditate quietly before bed. Meditate! A hell of a place to meditate in, I must say. He meditated himself to death through it, it seems."

"Never mind that, what did Keast say?"

"Only that just as we were due, the parson turned up and saw our light signals. Spotted Harry, too, flashed a light on him and asked him what he was doin' there at that time. The rest of the men with Harry cleared off. Harry said somethin' about him and his pals being there crabbing or fishing or something and about it being a good time there at high night-tide. Harry just had time to give us six flashes on his torch and our boats turned back. We dumped the stuff, too. Sharples played merry hell . . . "

"I'll bet he did. What happened then?"

"Well, the parson, I hear he was a bishop . . . "

"He was . . . ."

"The bishop havin' seen the lights started asking questions. Harry put him off, sayin' perhaps they could talk it over and come again another night just to make sure and not kick up a fuss without cause. So they arranged to say nothin' and come again to investigate. Harry said it was the best he could think up at the time, and it worked. He told me and Sharples. Next time we crossed somebody got the bishop there and brained him."

"Who?"

"Don't ask me. Keast didn't know, either. He didn't like it, I can damn well tell you and neither did I. Harry had his own ideas and must have tackled Sharples. The next thing, poor Harry got shot. I'm on the look-out for a fresh job, or *was.* Guess I'll not need one now for a bit . . . ."

"You're right there, Bradley."

"Anyhow, remember I came peaceable and I've done my best to help you now, haven't I?"

"Sure."

"You don't sound so certain . . . ."

"We want your help."

"Well . . . damn me! If that's not the limit. You want my help. Well, well . . . "

Littlejohn told Bradley what they wanted.

"Not much in that, anyhow. But remember when it comes to me in court, I gave it willingly. That a deal?"

"Right."

The gangway went out, the two remaining members of the crew went off the ship and were immediately collared by dock policemen. There was a confab. and then the men were allowed back to attend to the needs of the ship. They were the fire and enginemen and there were the boilers to be seen to. Below, the cattle, aware that land was near, were bellowing and stamping about in their stalls . . . .

The quay was dark, save for the riding-lights of the ships and the thin beams of distant lamps. The policemen had gone back to their little dock station. All was quiet except for the hiss of escaping steam and the noises of the cattle.

Suddenly a dark figure appeared at the gangway, slipped along it and stood on deck. Captain Bradley left the cabin, his figure silhouetted against the background of light within.

"That you, Bradley?"

"Yes. Who are you and what do you want? No business aboard till we're cleared by the customs."

"I'm Shearwater. You know me. I met you . . . ."

"Oh, yes. Well, what d'you want at this hour?"

"Can we go in your cabin. It's private . . . ."

The captain grunted and stood aside to let the man enter.

"Sit down. I've things to do first."

Bradley indicated the chair clamped beside the table and Shearwater sat down. Then the captain left him alone.

"Make yourself comfortable. I'll be about ten minutes. Then we'll talk," he threw back over his shoulder as he went.

Shearwater sat nervously at the table, casting his eyes round the cabin, fidgetting with the glass and bottle on the American leather cloth, putting his hands in his pockets and pulling them out again. He took a cigarette from his case and lit it . . . .

The door opened and closed again. Shearwater looked round.

He started.

"What are you doing here?"

It was O'Shaughnessy, but he had changed. He no longer wore his clerical suit and gold-framed glasses. Instead, he was dressed in loose-fitting tweeds with heavy shell spectacles on his nose.

"Didn't expect me, eh? I might ask you the same. Where have *you* been?"

The priestly benevolence had left him. There was no longer a mild look in his eyes, either. They seemed to have frozen to ice and shone with a relentless glacier light.

Shearwater looked uneasy.

"I came back to meet the *Patrick Creegan*. I'm scared, father. It's not safe over here. I'm getting off to Ireland as soon as I can and taking passage back to Africa. I've got mixed up in something that's too hot for me."

"Don't call me 'father' either. I'm sick of the mealy-mouthed rôle. I'm no more a parson than you are. You'd have guessed that if you'd had any wits."

"Are you going back with them this trip?" I am.

"I'll have company then . . . ."

O'Shaughnessy laughed. He seemed to enjoy the joke.

"No, you won't. I'm going on my own."

"What do you mean? I've fixed it already with the captain."

"Have you, now? Well, we won't trouble to unfix it, then. But you won't bother me much. You'll simply be cargo which we'll dump half way across . . . "

"What do you mean?"

"I mean this. Do you think I'm going to have you eternally in my hair for what you know about my affairs on this side. You gave me alibis when I needed them and I wouldn't be surprised if you've already told the police they were phoney. Have you?"

O'Shaughnessy strode to Shearwater, seized him roughly by the coat collar and shook him savagely.

"Here . . . You let me alone. How should I see the police? I've been on the run from them since I ran out of the hotel . . . ."

"So much the better. Though I don't believe you. Anyway, it's unlucky you're here and know me as I am without my glasses and clerical gear. I don't trust you, Shearwater, so I'll just have to put you where you're safe . . . ."

"Look here, I'm going. If you want to get away, I'll wait till the next boat. I'll hide somewhere . . . ."

"Too late. You know too much . . . ."

"What do I know?"

"Do you mean to tell me you didn't run out of the hotel because you got scared I'd do to you what I did to the bishop and Harry Keast . . . ."

"You mean . . . "

"Come on, you rat, you knew all along. You knew everybody had alibis but me and you knew I persuaded you to fake them for me. You tumbled to it and ran out before I dealt with you as I did the others . . . ." I never . . .

"Well, that's just too bad, because now I've got to shut your mouth. One shut mouth more or less doesn't make much difference."

Shearwater's face turned the colour of putty and he made for the door, but O'Shaughnessy was in the way, standing there with a small, blue automatic in his hand.

"You mean you killed the bishop and then Keast?"

"Who do you think did it? The yellow-livered Sharples? Or his gambling pals? Or perhaps you thought the Dean and Chapter did it to get him out of the way?"

"But why?"

"First the bishop stumbled across our men landing stuff. Keast, who seemed to have a bit of respect for his cloth, put him off the scent, but we'd no assurance that he wouldn't come prowling round again. We couldn't let him stand in the way of our new trade, now could we? Not after all the trouble we'd taken making arrangements and picking the right spot. Sharples got cold feet and was for moving our pitch or getting the bishop some way or other to stop prowling round. But the bishop was a stubborn man and kept on at Harry Keast to help him find out what was going on and then tell the police. So I arranged for Harry to send him a telephone message and bring him out next time we were there. I told Harry we'd call-off the trip that time and he could show the parson nothing was happening. I didn't call it off. Every trip's hundreds of pounds in our pocket. We weren't going to let a bloke nosing around in gaiters spoil it. I was there and coshed him on the head. Unluckily, the tide didn't wash away the body and Harry got tough about what I'd done. So Harry had to follow the bishop."

"So you shot Littlejohn, too?"

"I did. With the help of your alibi, I wanted to draw the scent off from Mervin to the bishop's home or Greyle. All of us at this end got alibis again, including me, with your kind help. If I let you go, you'll be straight off to the police and pin all this on me. I wish I'd got Littlejohn through the head instead of the leg, now. Then the local police would have still been combing the country round Cranage . . . ."

"I don't think so. You see, Littlejohn happens to have an assistant as keen as he is. You'd never have got away with it. In fact, you won't now."

"I shan't if I leave you loose. Otherwise, once in Eire, I'll find one of the old places and lie low till I can get safely away. I don't know why I'm telling you all this. But it gives me a certain amount of pleasure to see your surprise. You thought me a pious old fool, playing billiards with you and generally behaving mildly in between my little adventures . . . ."

"I've travelled all sorts of places, but I guess you're the most callous killer I ever met."

O'Shaughnessy's eyes blazed. He seemed to lose control of himself.

"Killing's never worried me since my father and elder brother were killed by your lot in The Trouble. Since then, no amount of treaties, milk-and-water peace talk or sentiment has stopped me carrying on the fight against the English. I helped the Germans in the war, and anybody who, by smuggling, racketeering, cheating or anything else is doing-down this blasted country will find me on his side. That's why I agreed to help Sharples and his gang. That and the money there was in it."

"But the rifle Littlejohn and Keast were shot with. We had no rifle with us . . . ."

"No. That's where my benevolent priestly air helped me. We followed Littlejohn just to see what he was at. When we found him nosing round Cranage, I got the idea that if he were attacked in the locality, interest would immediately be transferred there till we could clear things up at this end. When I left you, I followed him a bit and then saw a youth stalking rabbits with a rifle. I became a priest at once and gave him a lecture on cruelty to dumb animals. I knew that wouldn't carry any weight at all, but when I offered him twice the price he'd paid for the gun, his cupidity got the better of him. I bought the rifle from him just so's he shouldn't harm the little rabbits. I guess he went straight off and got another and pocketed the profit. But what are we waiting for? Bradley'll be back. I shall hide your body in one of the boats and you'll leave us somewhere on the Irish side, where you'll be washed up by the currents in a region where you'll not be known . . . ."

"I wouldn't do that if I were you, O'Rourke . . . ."

The curtain over the open porthole was drawn aside by a hand and Littlejohn's face appeared framed in the aperture. O'Shaughnessy raised his gun, but Cromwell, who had quickly entered by the door, knocked the weapon from the gunman's hand and caught him a blow on the point of the jaw, which dropped him unconscious.

"That's for what you did to the chief," he muttered, rubbing his knuckles with great satisfaction.

Chapter Twenty
The Last Game of Cards

SHARPLES entered the lounge first. Littlejohn was there already, smoking his pipe and watching the quayside. It was pouring with rain which, carried by the wind, swept along the pavement like a heavy mist. The *Patrick Creegan,* a thin wisp of steam escaping from her funnel, was still tied-up. Her decks were deserted.

"Morning," muttered Sharples. "Rotten weather we're having."

Littlejohn returned the greeting.

"Where are the regulars? There's generally a few about knitting and gossiping."

"Perhaps out."

Actually Littlejohn had arranged for Allain to keep the lounge clear of all except the gamblers. He didn't want an audience for the last hand.

Before they could continue the conversation a car drew up outside. Dr. Rooksby got out and rushed indoors to join his friend. Almost at once Hennessy and Wentworth followed.

"Hullo. Nobody about . . . ?"

Rooksby rubbed his hands and then glanced sheepishly at Littlejohn. He looked more uncomfortable still when

Cromwell entered, followed by Bowater. The newcomers took a seat in the window and, after a cursory nod to the rest, started to chat about the weather and the shipping down below.

"Care for a hand, Inspector? I'll stand down."

Sharples was very affable. He rang the bell, ordered drinks, produced a pack of cards and got ready for the usual game.

Littlejohn waved the offer aside.

"Let's all sit down. I want a talk with you gentlemen before you start playing. Bowater and Cromwell will be interested in this. Will you two join us, please?"

The card players had nothing to say. Sharples and Rooksby looked thoroughly alarmed, Hennessy annoyed and Wentworth slightly amused.

"What's all this about?" drawled Wentworth.

"Sit down and I'll tell you . . . ."

They scattered themselves in chairs round the table in their usual spots as if by force of habit. Cromwell took out a notebook and a stylo pen and started to write. Sharples glared at him.

"What's all this. If it's a police trick, I'll not stand for it. I want my lawyer."

"You'll see him soon enough, Mr. Sharples. I just want to tell you the *Patrick Creegan* put in here last night . . . ."

Sharples cackled nervously.

"That's a good one when we can see her right under our noses."

"Yes, isn't it? But this isn't so good. She put in with her *usual* cargo of nice things. Not only cattle, but cigarettes, stockings and other pleasant stuff . . . ."

Sharples jumped to his feet like a jack-in-the-box. Then he clutched the table and looked ready to faint. All the stuffing went out of Rooksby, who began to sweat visibly, a disgusting sight. Hennessy looked more annoyed than ever, and Wentworth didn't turn a hair.

Sharples spoke first.

"What's all this nonsense? Cigarettes, indeed. If there's any smuggling been going on, it's the crew, unknown to us . . . . We don't know anything. Do we?"

He appealed to the rest of his gang. Only Rooksby reacted.

"No, no. We know nothing."

Like a drowning man eagerly clutching at a straw.

Littlejohn stared straight ahead of him, watching the rain pouring down the window.

"Captain Bradley's in the local gaol. So is Father O'Shaughnessy, alias Martin O'Rourke. They've done their work and must pay for it. Now I'm concerned with those who started all this."

The room was utterly silent. Outside in the corridor the holidaymakers were noisily making the best of a bad job of weather. Fragments of conversation floated in.

"If it's like this this afternoon, I shall go to bed . . . ."

"Is there a matinée at the pictures . . . ?"

"It's a funny thing when the glass says 'Fair,' it always rains and when it says 'Stormy,' it's a lovely day. Must be something wrong with it . . . ."

Up above, the roar and hum of a vacuum cleaner.

The barmaid thrust in her head.

"You gentlemen any orders?"

Nobody answered, she looked astonished and then disappeared nonplussed.

"A small line of packet-boats presents an easy chance for smuggling . . . ."

Littlejohn was still gazing through the window.

" . . . Especially on a coast like this, with a ready-made ideal landing-place like Bolter's Hole. Perhaps the owners of the boat didn't think of it. Perhaps they did. Anyhow, somebody from Eire saw glorious chances as the duties on tobacco and such soared and as the black markets clamoured for things plentiful in Eire but strictly on coupons over here."

Dr. Rooksby had his face in his hands as though trying to shut out the truth. Hennessy actually started to write in a little notebook himself. He looked up unpleasantly at Littlejohn and spat a string of words at him.

"I warn you, Inspector, I'll not stand for this sort of talk. We're not going to have a scandal pinned on us. Whatever others may have done unknown to us, we've kept our company free from reproach. Haven't we Sharples?"

Sharples didn't seem to hear.

"Haven't we, Sharples?"

Hennessy was getting annoyed.

"Oh yes, yes . . . "

"In that case I'm taking notes which I shall hand to our lawyer . . . ."

Wentworth threw back his head and laughed loudly.

"What are you laughing at? There's nothing funny as far as I can see . . . ."

"Just Sharples' face . . . ."

"Whether the company started it or not, I don't know. But soon an agent in Eire, an ex-gunman called O'Rourke, was regularly sending stuff across on the *Patrick Creegan.* They were loaded off the Irish coast and then unloaded into the ship's boats here and put ashore at Bolter's Hole. They then found their way down to your warehouses, Mr. Sharples . . . ."

"It's a lie . . . I . . . "

"Please don't carry on this farce any longer, Sharples. The police were in your cellars just before I came in. They've impounded everything."

Hennessy sprang to his feet and seized Sharples by the throat.

"Why, you little swine. What have you been at with our boat? Why wasn't I told . . . ?"

Wentworth yawned.

"Your integrity, Hennessy, stands so high in the town. And what's more, it's genuine. Not like Sharples', just a façade for a lot of crooked work behind it. Sharples and Rooksby knew they'd bust the whole show if they approached you. You'd not stand for it. Not that I'm in this. I'm small fry for Sharples. Not energetic and shady enough. He and Rooksby found the capital, I guess. You and I were the stooges, the respectable alibis for the rest. Hey! Lily! Bring drinks round. Sharples and Rooksby look to need them and a drink for the rest won't do any harm."

The barmaid quickly brought the order and scuttered out again, scared by the ominous looks on the faces of the men.

"Go on, Inspector," added Wentworth. "What next?"

Littlejohn didn't touch his drink, but lit his pipe.

"Sharples had an arrangement with the watchman on the quayside. There's a road-widening scheme been going on there which has been abandoned, but our friend in his capacity as chairman of the Highways Committee had arranged for the site to be watched and lamps strung round it at night. The order of these lamps, which are visible at sea, told Bradley on the *Patrick Creegan* whether or not the coast was clear. Any sudden emergency and the order of the lamps was changed, the contraband was jettisoned and the *Patrick Creegan* sailed in normally."

"Now, had the Customs been alert in the port, it might not have been so easy. As it is, Dunblow, the chief official, is just hanging on for his pension and doesn't care a hoot. Provided he keeps a check on incoming goods at the port, he never bothers about the rest of the coast. So it was simple . . . ."

Rooksby having swallowed his drink, grew bold.

"I know nothing about all this. I want my lawyer. I shall protest . . . "

Sharples rose livid with fury.

"You're in this just as much as I am and you'll go through all I've got coming with me. I guess you'll say you were joking when you put the idea in my head. You were always hard-up and ready for easy ways of making money on the sly . . . ."

"Be quiet, you two. You'll have a chance to settle all this later. Your scheme worked a little while and then a bishop arrived who'd some strange freaks about meditation and he took to prowling the coast round Bolter's Hole. He caught your men at it and you'd the devil's own work keeping him from going to the police at once. His interference for the first time caused Harry Keast to panic, give the signal for retreat and cause Bradley to jettison several hundred pounds' worth of stuff. I guess you reported it by telephone to your man, O'Rourke, who came over hot-foot. Perhaps you didn't know, perhaps you did, but he was an ex-gunman who'd stop at nothing. Well-known to the Dublin police who'd lost track of him and who's served a stretch or two for things like robbery with violence. He came over here at once, dressed-up as a priest on holiday. Rather an ingenious way of allaying suspicion . . . ."

Sharples turned green.

"I knew nothing about that. I'd nothing to do with murdering anybody."

"All the same, you made yourself an accessory, because you knew of the crime and guessed who'd done it. Yet you never told the police . . . Lily! Get some brandy for Mr. Sharples, he's not well . . . "

Sharples eagerly drank off the order.

"O'Rourke, calling himself O'Shaughnessy, saw that if he didn't act quickly the whole scheme would bust and the police would be after the lot of you. Reckless, as usual, he arranged for Keast to decoy the bishop down to Bolter's Hole and there pushed him over the cliffs, after knocking him on the head. But just in case the police got too importunate, he provided himself with an alibi. He tacked on to Shearwater, a harmless sort of fellow, and had the nerve to tell him he was an amateur detective investigating smuggling or something and anxious to get a step ahead of the police. Shearwater believed his tale and good-humouredly provided false alibis. After the telephone call which got the bishop to Bolter's Hole, O'Shaughnessy hurried Shearwater to bed, and then pretended to go to his own room. He realistically took off his boots for the night porter to collect and clean and not having another pair, had to help himself to some from another room. He chose Cuhady's . . . ."

Wentworth roared.

"Well . . . My God! I must send Cuhady a postcard about this. He'll be tickled to death to hear of O'Shaughnessy's trick. The priest was the one who quietened him off by some sort of spiritual comfort . . . ."

"Will you stop laughing . . . . This isn't funny. It's damned awful . . . ."

Hennessy, too, had lost all his spirits and sagged in his chair.

"Keast got conscience-stricken about the murder of the bishop, so O'Rourke had to silence him. He took a shot at me, too, with a rifle he bought from a lad in the country and later hid in the luggage-boot of Shearwater's car. We've found it there. O'Rourke left it to throw suspicion on Shearwater if it were discovered . . . ."

"I knew nothing about all this . . . ."

Sharples was pawing the air like a madman.

"You can tell that to the magistrates . . . . At any rate, you were so greedy for gain that you pooh-poohed Captain

Bradley's caution. With the police around, he didn't want to ship contraband at all, but you insisted. You thought us too dumb to guess what you were at. Then Shearwater vanished and you didn't hear of it till too late to stop the shipment by 'phone at the Irish side. Instead, you got Jeale, the watchman, to give the alarm on his lamps. We saw that the wrong signal was given and caught the *Patrick Creegan* at it red-handed."

"What's going to happen to the company, now?" said Hennessy. He was beginning to think of his own money.

"Oh, shut-up, you. You and your damned money. As if we hadn't enough . . . "

"For two pins, Sharples, I'd break your blasted neck . . . ."

Wentworth laughed.

"The hangman'll do it for you. He's an accessory . . . ."

They had to give Sharples some more brandy.

"We managed to get hold of Shearwater before O'Rourke got at him. He'd certainly have killed him if he could, because Shearwater had the power to smash all O'Rourke's alibis and put the rope round his neck. Shearwater fell in with our scheme. We had him dodge up to the hotel on the pretext of borrowing some money from Allain and then Allain on the way to the safe just whispered to O'Rourke who was, as usual, keeping out of the limelight in the billiard room. That put O'Rourke on Shearwater's trail. He followed him to the *Patrick Creegan* where Shearwater was to pretend to bargain for a passage with the captain to Eire. Bradley, hoping to mitigate his own punishment, helped us, too, and left Shearwater alone in his cabin, with three of us listening at an open porthole. O'Rourke wasn't long in taking his chance. He went to kill Shearwater and throw him overboard as the ship made her way back to Eire, for he didn't know we'd caught them smuggling and that Bradley was under arrest.

In a fit of bravado, egged on by Shearwater, rather pluckily, I think, O'Rourke told the whole tale. We kept it all dark until now, just so that we could see the reactions of you four gentlemen. There's no doubt about you and Rooksby, Sharples . . . ."

He nodded to Bowater, who had been quietly taking it all in, looking thirstily at his drink, yet not daring to touch it because he considered himself on duty. Cromwell, having taken his revenge on O'Rourke for shooting Littlejohn, looked very pleased with himself.

Bowater cleared his throat and rose.

"Arthur Wellesley Sharples, I arrest you . . . "

Then he called a constable from outside and turned to Rooksby to read a warrant to him.

Doctor Rooksby fainted.

The pair of them had to be carried to the waiting taxi, thereby causing an exciting finish to a rainy, boring morning for the visitors who had stayed indoors.

"And I must ask you two gentlemen kindly to stay in town. We shall need you . . . ."

"It'll be a pleasure," said Hennessy.

"I shan't stir," drawled Wentworth. "But I wonder if you and Bowater would like to make up a four at cards now and then. I don't know how I'm going to pass the time . . . ."

A week later Wentworth was taken to a private asylum. It seems he'd been going that way for a long time. Hennessy entered into the prosecution of his former colleagues with the greatest relish.

O'Rourke was hanged and Bradley and Sharples got long terms of imprisonment. Rooksby didn't even come before the local magistrates. He hanged himself on his shoelaces the night he was arrested. The strain of the case so upset Bowater that he had a brief breakdown which placed him at the tender mercies of Dr. Tordopp, who gave him such hell that he was well and about again more quickly than is usual in such cases.

In spite of the need for a longer holiday and the willingness of Scotland Yard to grant it, Littlejohn went home and recovered quickly after spending sunny days on Hampstead Heath near his home. He passed a lot of time seated on the grass in the sun and air, reading detective stories, which are one of his favourite diversions. They appeal to his irrepressible sense of humour.

The Case of the Demented Spiv

George Bellairs

Chapter One
The Demented Spiv

AT the Oddfellows' Arms, Brockfield, they had come to the end of a perfect day and with the help of Drake and his merry, merry men had laid the enemy low. Or rather Jack Stansfield had done it with the assistance of several pints of beer, a tinny piano and a reedy tenor voice. To mark their approval the occupants of the bar parlour clapped unanimously or banged their pots on the beery table-tops, and one occupant, half-seas-over, emptied his glass in the piano in gratitude for its share in the victory.

It was an October Saturday night and raining cats and dogs outside. That hadn't kept the regulars away, of course. The crack of doom couldn't have done that. But the casuals were missing and that irritated the landlord. He almost struck the man who'd lubricated the piano, but the offender was silly with drink and kept on grinning and saying it was a "good ole pianner." What can you do with anyone like that? But it caused an awkward lull in the good-feeling for a bit. They asked Stansfield to sing an encore and after a florid introduction, played by ear by the paid accompanist, he started "Absent."

Sometimes, between long shadows on the grass. . . .

It floated out feebly into the deserted street and made the solitary policeman, standing under a gas-lamp, his cape shining like jet with the rain, wish he were in the warm, steamy pub instead of outside. He'd still four hours of this to endure. The red lamp on the top of the police-box nearby began to twinkle and he hurried to answer the telephone in the cupboard underneath it. Some children had been letting off fireworks prematurely and were keeping an old lady on tenterhooks waiting for the next bang. He'd better go and see about it.

"Very good. . . . I'll go. . . . "

Nothing exciting ever happened in Brockfield. A few drunks, kids with fireworks, cats left in lock-up shops over week-end, stray dogs. . . . The constable sighed. He was fed-up.

The church next door to the Oddfellows' Arms was a blaze of light. They were holding a revivalist rally. Brockfield has more pubs and churches per square mile than any other town in England. Any of the burgesses will tell you that. Of course, other towns boast the same thing, but we can't waste time refuting it. The fact was that the big, well-illuminated church was full of people and they couldn't begin the service because the organist was missing. The deputy organist was laid-up with lumbago, too, and they were in a fix. The only other person who could play was the preacher himself, and as it was quite impossible to work the people up satisfactorily without a rousing hymn beforehand, the parson had to keep leaving the pulpit, playing a verse or two and then hurrying back to say what he had to say before the congregation went off the boil. It was hard work. Everyone was annoyed with the fugitive organist, to say the least of it. Strains of Drake and his merry, merry men and Absent floated in now and then from the Oddfellows' next door, and they had to close the windows on that side, although the church was like an oven from congestion.

Rain lashed the street as the dripping constable returned to his stand under the gas-lamp. He had effectively silenced the young pyrotechnicians, who, on account of the rain, had been lighting their thunder-flashes under their jackets and then throwing them into convenient dustbins to go off. Now the bobby had nothing to do but get wet. He longed for a drunken brawl to break out, or even a serious road accident. Anything where he could behave with efficiency and earn a pat on the back from his superior officers, who were beginning to regard the hush of law and order in the town with suspicion. The police always missing when they were wanted, so to speak. As if P.C. 132 could help it. . . .

Now they were singing "Abide with me" in the church and the strains having reached the Oddfellows', the occupants of the bar parlour took it up, and chapel and pub side by side echoed the same hymn. P.C. 132 stopped his troubled thinking to listen and said to himself it sounded very nice and that people weren't always as pagan as you thought they were. . . .

Suddenly, like a bolt from the blue, trouble invaded the sodden, silent street. A closed van with headlamps full on, dazzling the eyes until they pained, and lighting up the floods of water rushing to the gutters, zigzagged dangerously down the incline of shining cobblestones and pulled-up with a frightful squeal of brakes in front of the Oddfellows' Arms. The door opened and was closed again with a bang and a flying figure ran into the pub. P.C. 132 ponderously crossed the road and began to examine the vehicle. . . .

"Give me a double brandy," the newcomer was saying inside the inn. Unable to find anyone at the little bar at one end of the long corridor which led from the vestibule, he had opened the door of the bar parlour.

At the sight of him, the occupants suddenly stopped singing. Some of them left their mouths open in surprise, the song suddenly cut off from them.

"Give me a double brandy. . . . "

"We haven't any," said the landlord, still in a bad temper. He had some hidden away for special occasions but he wasn't serving it to any Tom, Dick or Harry who had the cheek to call on the off-chance and ask for a double.

"Give me anything. . . . "

"Only rum. . . . "

"For God's sake . . . Rum . . . Anything. . . . "

The man looked in a state of collapse. He was wet through and bare-headed. His dark, long hair was so heavily oiled that the rain formed in globules on it and ran down his face and back instead of soaking in. Narrow slits of eyes, a thin, long, pointed nose, and a fleshy-lipped mouth with a streak of dark moustache across the top of it. Dazzled by the light and apparently thrown into confusion by some unknown terror, he grimaced and twitched like an idiot. The rain ran from his clothes and formed a pool round his feet. . . .

The customers of the pub looked hard at him and summed him up. A cheapjack, a street-corner boy, the sort who stood on the local open-air market selling odds and ends of jewellery, and, on the sly, clothing coupons. They gave him the collective cold-shoulder at once. They were all honest-to-goodness working folk and there was no place for an easy-money boy among them. They eyed his clothes with disdain. Heavy overcoat of light cloth, with high padded shoulders and waist pinched in like a pair of corsets; limp, soaked, baggy trousers escaping from beneath the coat and falling low on a pair of long, brown pointed-toed shoes. The trembling hand holding the double rum was long and mean, but the finger-nails were effeminately manicured. . . .

"Give me another. . . . "

The landlord reluctantly did so. The chap was so obviously all-in, it seemed a kindness to do it. Especially after singing a hymn. . . .

The outer door opened and closed and P.C. 132 stood with his huge back to it, taking all in before enquiring what it was all about.

"Spiv. . . . "

One of the party more impudent than the rest and made bold by beer, uttered the word like an expectoration. The rest sniggered and looked pleased at the joke.

The word seemed like the last straw to the strange figure in the padded coat. He removed the glass, from which he was gulping, from his mouth with a gesture so quick that it spilled the contents half-way across the room.

"Spiv, did you say . . . ?"

The man who had been bold, braced himself against the wall behind his chair as though expecting a sudden assault.

"Spiv. . . . Yes, I am a spiv. That's what they all say. They stop in the street and shout it after me. Well, they're right. I am a spiv. I'm a spiv . . . spiv . . . spiv. . . . "

He shouted the word as though it pleased him, like someone who has earned a degree or received a title mouthing it to himself with deep satisfaction. He stood there, the rain dripping from him, his slits of eyes now widened and round, terror in every line of his body.

"'ere, 'ere, what's all this?"

The huge figure of the law stood in the doorway. Everyone sighed with relief. They didn't quite know how to deal with the situation. P.C. 132 looked ready for anything.

"What's all this?"

The newcomer turned and faced the officer.

"I'm a spiv. . . . "

"Well, now, who'd have thought it?"

The bobby was being heavily jocular, but the man in the waisted overcoat was deadly serious.

"Yes. . . . But whatever I've done, I never killed anybody. I didn't do it. . . . I swear I didn't. . . . "

The constable stiffened and towered over the man.

"Who says anybody's killed somebody?" he said in his best constabulary style.

"I didn't do it. . . . He was dead when I got there. . . . "

The drinkers round the fire were petrified. They all sat there like the cast of "The Sleeping Beauty" struck immobile by the witch's curse.

"Where've you come from and what you been doin'?"

"Fennings' Mill. . . . I didn't do it. . . . "

The constable placed a warning hand on the stranger's shoulder and it seemed that that was all that was needed to crack him up altogether. As though the huge paw were a ton in weight, the man crumpled under it, sank to the tiled floor and sat there talking to himself.

"He was dead, staring at me. I didn't do it. I'm not a murderer; I'm only a spiv. . . . "

The embarrassed bobby stooped with difficulty, for his cape and his paunch impeded any bending movement, and tried to raise the man.

"He's gone off his rocker," said someone.

There was a murmur of general assent.

The constable looked angrily at the figure on the floor, jerked back his helmeted head as though seeking guidance from heaven, and then rubbed his chin with the back of his hand.

"I'm phonin' for help," he said. "You lot look after 'im till I get back."

And he stamped purposefully out and across to the police-box. Something was happening with a vengeance now!

Back at the inn, the occupants of the bar parlour, men and women, were on their feet and had gathered round the stranger, like participants in a parlour game. The man on the floor was sitting there, fully conscious, talking to himself an unintelligible gibberish, but in a tone of self-comfort and excuse.

Two more constables soon arrived and the little posse picked up the spiv, carried him out, dumped him in his own van and drove him to the police station, where, in due course, the surgeon with the concurrence of a colleague, certified him as having the balance of his mind disturbed, to say the least of it, and committed him to the asylum under police guard.

"Better have a look at Fennings' Mill and see what he's been at," said the Inspector on duty to P.C. 132 after hearing his report. "Expect it's just a mad tale, but we'd better look round."

Fennings' Mill was an old stone factory, chiefly engaged in weaving cotton for shirtings, and stood just behind the police station. It was approached by a maze of narrow streets, terminating in a large walled croft on which stood the mill, with dumps for coal, packing cases, warehouses and a small reservoir for the engines, surrounding it.

There was no watchman on duty, but the constables found the iron gates which broke the surrounding wall wide open.

"Hullo," said P.C. 132 gruffly.

"Hullo," said his colleague, 124, in another key.

"So there 'as been somethin' up!"

"Looks like it."

There was a gas-lamp burning near the gates. It threw long shadows down the alley and illuminated a few scuttering rats. Otherwise there was nobody about. The rain was still coming down in torrents. A real night for keeping people indoors.

The constables turned on their torches and cautiously walked across the cobblestoned mill-yard. All was still. The first building was a block of stone offices, single-storied, the lower halves of its windows covered in gauze screens with W. & H. J. Fenning, Ltd., printed across them in gilt. The bobbies tried the doors, which they found locked.

Next, the main entrance to the mill itself. Doors locked here, too. No signs of disturbance at all. Then the boiler-house, where they fired the great furnaces to drive the engine. This was secure and safe behind its drawn steel shutters. Beyond, you could hear the crackle of the fires, damped down for the week-end. Steam hissed somewhere, gently like a distant angry snake. Otherwise, not a sound.

"Urn," said P.C. 132.

"Aye," assented 124.

"Better try the warehouse. Looks like a false alarm."

They tramped across the yard to the square, two-storied block which held the raw yarn and the finished products awaiting delivery.

The door was open!

The two policemen entered shoulder to shoulder, as though expecting a massed attack of startled intruders. All was quiet, however, but on the floor, about a dozen paces from the door, lay a figure, staring at the ceiling. The open eyes and the livid face gave the constables quite a turn. They groaned with surprise.

"Jeepers!" said 124.

"Wot?" said 132.

"I only said 'Jeepers'."

P.C. 132, his mind momentarily removed from the horror at his feet by his comrade's strange utterance, looked puzzled and then switched back to business.

"Bin strangled by the looks of it. . . . "

"'orrible. . . . "

"I'll say. Better ring-up the station. Is that a 'phone in that corner over there?"

Whilst his colleague telephoned for help, P.C. 132 knelt with an effort and cautiously examined the body.

"We found a dead body 'ere in Fennings' warehouse. Yes, stone dead. Strangled by the look o' things. Very good, sir. . . . "

"Hey, look at this," shouted P.C. 132 to P.C. 124.

"What? . . . Who is he?"

"I don't know. But look at this."

With a heavy finger the constable indicated the upper lip of the corpse. It was covered by a large dark moustache, obviously a false one. The constable touched the cheeks, too, and then looked at his finger under the light of his lamp.

"Theatrical paint!" he murmured as though to himself. "He's disguised himself or somethin'. . . . "

"Rum go, isn't it?"

"I know that face. Seen it before somewhere. Now. . . . "

The policeman pondered and then, suddenly growing impatient, bent and pulled off the false moustache.

"Got to come off anyhow. Might as well," he said as though excusing himself to himself.

"See who it is? See who it is?"

P.C. 124 was almost beside himself with the delight of discovery.

"Why, it's Ambrose Barrow, secretary of this 'ere mill."

"Right you are, Joe."

"No wonder they was runnin' about like a lot of loonies at Hake Street Chapel to-night. He's organist there and they've some sort o' special service on. Put 'em in queer street when he didn't turn up."

"I'll bet it did, Joe. And them little thinkin' he was lyin' here, dead. Strangled. . . . "

"I wonder if that spiv done it."

The two policemen drew closer together. It was eerie in the dim light, with the rain dripping monotonously outside and the rush of water in the gutters overhead. Somewhere, the yowling of a cat split the air. Rats were scuttering about on the floor above.

"No wonder 'e went potty and they had to put him away," said P.C. 132.

"I'll say," answered his mate.

Want another Perfect Mystery?

Get your next Classic Crime Story for FREE ...

Sign up to our Crime Classics newsletter where you can discover new Golden Age crime, receive exclusive content and never-before published short stories, all for FREE.

From the beloved greats of the golden age to the forgotten gems, best-kept-secrets, and brand new discoveries, we're devoted to classic crime.

If you sign up today, you'll get:

1. A Free Novel from our Classic Crime collection.
2. Exclusive insights into classic novels and their authors and the chance to get copies in advance of publication, and
3. The chance to win exclusive prizes in regular competitions.

Interested? It takes less than a minute to sign up. You can get your novel and your first newsletter by signing up on our website www.crimeclassics.co.uk

22171160R00122

Printed in Great Britain
by Amazon